THE CRESCENT AND THE

CROSS

THE CRESCENT AND THE CROSS

ROBERT ROGLAND

The Crescent and the Cross: The Eighth Voyage of Sinbad

PUBLISHED BY:
Grace & Truth Books
815 Exchange Ave., Ste. 101
Conway, AR 72032
www.graceandtruthbooks.com
918.245.1500

Printed in the United States of America
ISBN: 978-1-960297-00-6

Contents

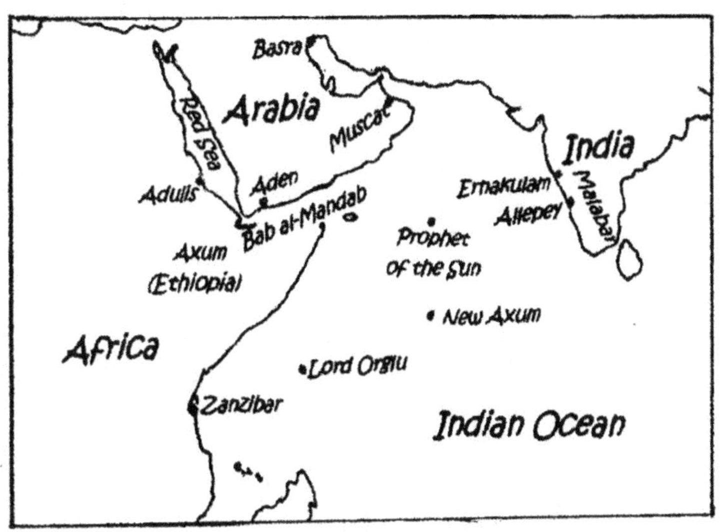

Sinbad's Ports of Call

The reader is invited to trace Sinbad's voyage with the aid of this map.

Chapter 1
Sinbad Goes on Pilgrimage

Raging waves tossed me back and forth like a cat playing with a mouse. I clung desperately to a few waterlogged planks, all that was left of my dinghy. How long could my weary fingers hang on? The storm would not blow itself out before morning. By then, hungry fish would have consumed my lifeless carcass with relish, and nothing but a few bones would remain of Sinbad the Sailor. I had challenged the sea seven times and won each challenge. Now the sea would finally conquer.

But no! God delivered me from the hungry sea and a dozen other terrifying perils that followed on my eighth, most extraordinary voyage. Out of gratitude to God, I must tell you my story.

I imagine you've read of the many adventures and misfortunes I suffered on my earlier voyages. The Caliph of Baghdad, Haroun al-Rashid the Great, had my story recorded in the annals of the court for the entertainment and wonder of his subjects. That story has spread beyond his domain to lands over the sea. But if you know only my first seven voyages, you know only the smallest part of my adventures. My eighth voyage, unknown to the world till now, surpassed them all. I passed through the most horrifying dangers, saw the most astounding marvels, and brought home the richest of treasures, a treasure that will outlast death! On that voyage, I met my dearest friend. His name is Selassie. The story I am going to tell is his as well as mine.

After the harrowing dangers of my seventh voyage, I resolved never to go to sea again but to live a life of luxury and ease. Indeed, the best of all futures lay before me. I was then a Muslim. I had already made my confession that Muhammad was the messenger of Allah, I prayed toward Mecca five times a day, I fasted during the month of Ramadan, and I was wealthy enough to give generously to the poor and still deny myself no pleasure. I could fulfill all the obligations of a good Muslim and still live life to the full.

And live life to the full I did! I dwelled in a marble palace on the banks of the Tigris River. Every day I rose late from my bed of satin cushions and silk sheets. After morning prayers, I would breakfast on dates, pomegranates, and soft, warm rolls served on a silver plate. Then I would plan my day as I sat on my riverfront terrace sipping thick, rich Yemeni coffee from a golden cup.

After breakfast, I would give my household steward his orders for the day. Then other slaves would carry me in a litter into the heart of the city, where I visited the moneylenders who managed my fortune. While in the city, I also took care to give alms to beggars every day, for I wanted to earn favor with Allah.

By lunchtime, I was home. I said my noon prayers and retired to the terrace, where the midday meal was waiting. Perhaps it would be roast peacock, perhaps lamb braised in a hot Indian curry—whatever I craved was mine. Musicians and dancers entertained me while I ate. After I had dined, I would retire to my bedroom for a nap in the heat of the day. A slave would fan me with an ostrich plume while I slept.

My slave would wake me in mid-afternoon at the third hour of prayer. After I finished my prayers, I would find my bath drawn—not too hot, not too cold, with rose petals scattered over the surface. After I bathed, a slave trimmed my beard and nails and laid out fresh clothes. I then spent an hour reading and meditating on the Koran, the book Muhammad claimed he received from Allah. I would conclude my devotions by praying at the fourth hour appointed for prayer.

I gave every evening over to parties and feasting. My slaves were busy during the day, inviting friends and business partners to supper. My guests would begin to arrive at dusk. We would feast, converse, and enjoy the musicians and dancers long after the star-spangled night had settled over Baghdad, the Abode of Peace. When the last guest had gone home, I would say my evening prayers and retire to bed. So I passed my days for two years, refusing myself nothing while still carrying out the duties of a faithful Muslim.

Yet as the months passed, my heart was troubled more and more about my eternal destiny. I began to wonder if I was good enough to merit paradise. The Koran said Allah could do whatever he wanted. No one could question his ways or call him to account. The Koran said he was merciful and good, but he could cast me into hell at a whim if it struck his fancy. I hoped he would look on me with favor if my good deeds outnumbered my bad deeds, but I was never sure they did, no matter how often I gave alms in the streets or helped widows and orphans in their poverty.

The more I thought on these things, the emptier my riches seemed. I gave to the poor more freely than before, but my anxiety grew. I was no longer a young man. All too soon, I would die, and then what? Would my good deeds outweigh my bad deeds in the eyes of the Almighty on the fearful Day of Judgment?

One Friday, I went to the mosque, as was my custom. The sermon dealt with the five pillars of Islam, the duties Allah demands of faithful Muslims. As the imam preached, it struck me that I had performed only four of the five pillars. I had not made the pilgrimage to Mecca that the Koran requires of every Muslim who can afford it. Of course! That was why I felt my righteousness was insufficient to please Allah. I resolved then and there to become a Hajji, a Muslim who has made his pilgrimage.

That evening my closest friends and relations came to dine with me as usual. After supper, I sent the musicians and dancers away and motioned for silence.

"Friends, I have an important announcement to make. I will be going on pilgrimage tomorrow. I have placed the management of my affairs in the hands of Hassan, my elder brother. *Inshallah*, God willing, I will return home in six months."

All were speechless at first; then, they burst out in shouts of congratulations and best wishes. Every good Muslim wants to go on pilgrimage, but not all can afford to make the journey. They rejoiced with me, and all begged me to pray for them while I was in Mecca. I assured them I would do so. I called the musicians and dancers back, and while they entertained, I spent the rest of the evening talking with my guests about my plans for the trip. When they departed, well after midnight, I sent them all away with rich gifts.

The next morning, I donned a simple pilgrim's garb and filled my bag with a plentiful supply of gold sequins. I boarded a riverboat for Basra, on the Persian Gulf. I knew Basra well, for it was from Basra that I had departed on all my voyages. There I hoped to find a pilgrim ship headed for Arabia.

Many pilgrim ships departed from Basra every year, but it was not the pilgrim season. I was so anxious to fulfill my obligation to Allah that I couldn't wait six months till the yearly hajj began—I hoped to be home by then! Since pilgrim ships were not yet sailing, I had to settle for a dhow, a merchant vessel going first to Muscat, on the Omani coast of Arabia, and then to Jeddah, on the Red Sea. From Jeddah, I would travel by caravan over the coastal mountains to Mecca.

I didn't mind laying over in Muscat for a few days. A great slave market ran year-round in Muscat, and I needed a personal servant. Abdullah, the boy who had been my attendant since I returned from my seventh voyage, had run away just a week earlier. Ungrateful wretch! No matter; the loss of a slave meant little to a man as wealthy as I. One slave was as good as another—or so I thought.

Chapter 2
The New Slave

Muscat was a ten-day sail from Basra if the weather was favorable, and favorable it was: surely Allah was blessing my pilgrimage! The Persian Gulf was smooth and calm. Delicate tracings of foam curled lazily on the face of the gleaming water, looking for all the world like a tray of Damascus silver with engravings swirling all over its surface. The sun glared down from a cloudless sky, but a steady breeze kept the temperature bearable and filled the sails of the ship as it glided south at a steady clip. As I stood in the bow and drew in breath after breath of fresh sea air, I was surprised at the joy welling up in me. Ah, to be at sea again! I had not realized how much I missed having a deck under my feet. Perhaps, I mused, I would even resume my travels after I returned from pilgrimage.

In eight days, we passed through the Strait of Hormuz, out of the Persian Gulf, and into the Indian Ocean. The water remained calm, and the breeze never slackened. I ate, prayed, and slept on deck, rejoicing in the sea and sky. Two days after entering the Indian Ocean, I awoke to see the dark mountains of the Omani coast looming in front of me. I took the helmsman's glass and scanned the beach where the mountains plunged into the sea. Soon I could make out the whitewashed buildings of Muscat gleaming in the morning sun.

We docked at noon. After prayers, I set off for the slave market. I had been in Muscat many times before and knew right where to go: past the shipyard, past the India docks, all the way to the north end of town. A twenty-minute walk brought me to the Bazaar of Slaves. It had not changed since I was there ten years before. A half-dozen toughs, armed with curved, razor-sharp scimitars, lounged around the gate. They were supposed to be on guard, but they looked bored and inattentive. And why not? Not once in the memory of any man living had a slave ever made a break for freedom. The guards were slaves themselves, but they had an easy life and knew it.

Inside the gate, I found myself in a square open to the scorching sky. Single-story warehouses with barred windows surrounded the courtyard. In front of each building stood a platform raised four feet or so above the surface of the ground. There the slavers displayed their human merchandise. Canny buyers and eager sellers, all shouting and making deals, crowded around the platforms. Only the slaves were silent. Who would they talk to? They would have been captured only a few months earlier. Few would be from the same tribe, and few would know Arabic. The poor wretches sat quietly behind the platforms until their owner, with a wave of his hand, would order them up on the block

I sauntered down one side of the market and back up the other. When I had located the healthiest batch of slaves, I approached them to make my choice. I saw the boy I wanted right away. He was African, probably Ethiopian or Nubian, like most of the slaves there. His bearing impressed me immediately. Most children hunched in fear or cried when forced to mount the platform; those too young or too dull to know what was happening might act silly or embarrassed. But this lad was different; he stood erect and carried himself with calm dignity. He looked healthy, too. I stopped in front of him and looked him up and down.

"Open your mouth, boy; let me see your teeth," I ordered.

"Yes, my lord," he replied in slightly accented Arabic, and showed me a perfect set of teeth. So he knew Arabic already! This boy was definitely the one I wanted to purchase.

The boy did not go cheap, but his owner and I agreed on a fair price, considering the lad's age, health, and the fact that he could take orders in Arabic immediately. Next, we headed to the clothing bazaar to buy him proper apparel. Slaves at the market wear no more than a loincloth, hardly acceptable attire for a slave of Sinbad! Soon we were on our way back to the ship. I strode along in front while the boy trotted respectfully behind me, clothed in a simple white cotton tunic and embroidered skullcap, an outfit befitting his master.

Back at the ship, I told the boy that I expected him to have my meals and coffee ready at the appointed time, to shave me after breakfast, and to wash my clothes daily so that he would have fresh garments to lay out for me every morning.

"You'll cook and clean for yourself also, of course. You're to look clean, neat, and worthy of being the slave of Sinbad. You'll have other regular duties after we dock in Jeddah, but that will be enough while we're aboard ship. Of course, I'll have special orders for you from time to time. Carry out your duties loyally and efficiently, and you'll find me to be a kind, even generous master. Dishonesty and laziness will bring my wrath upon you. Do you understand?"

"Yes, my lord. I hope to give you good service."

"Fairly spoken, but I'll discover soon enough if your service lives up to your words."

At that moment, the captain appeared on deck and announced that we would be sailing in an hour. Sailing in an hour! We were supposed to stay in Muscat for two more days.

"Why are we leaving so soon?" I asked.

"I have seen an omen in the heavens that tells me the monsoon will arrive early this year. Today's sky may be blue and cloudless, but this morning I saw four terns circling over the harbor. Other skippers think I'm a superstitious old salt who ought to give up sailing, but I believe in bird signs. Four terns mean there will be four more weeks before the weather turns bad. May it please Allah to spare mariners then! We've got to get out of the open ocean before the monsoon begins. If we sail today, we'll be at the Bab al-Mandab in a month. Once we pass through it into the Red Sea, we can find a sheltered harbor if we need one. We have just enough time if we sail today." I knew enough not to argue with a captain who believed in bird signs. Besides, I too had been surprised by tempests that swept down without warning and wrecked my ship (you have read about my seven voyages, haven't you?).

"Take no chances," I told the captain. "Play it safe." Of course, the sooner I got to Jeddah, the sooner I'd get to Mecca, so our early departure was good news to me in every way.

After sunset, some miles off the coast and heading southwest under a sky sparkling with stars, I finally had a chance to talk more with my new slave. He had cooked and served me supper, had boiled and poured my coffee, and was busy washing up when I sat down on the deck in front of him and began to ask questions.

"I'm surprised you know Arabic, lad. When did you learn it?"

"I learned it traveling with my father, lord."

"Was your father a merchant?"

"No, lord, he was a military man."

"Ah, then you were captured in a tribal war."

"More or less, lord," the boy replied. "My father was on a secret mission, with only four men and me, when a band of slavers fell upon us."

"And your father? Was he killed or captured?"

"I don't know, lord. We were attacked at night, and I was carried off in the confusion. I don't know. Oh, lord, I miss my family so!" The boy was hardly able to get the last sentence out before he began to sob.

"Don't cry, boy," I said, patting him on the back. "I know it's hard; I was orphaned myself at an early age. I'm no substitute for a father, of course, but you'll find me a kind master, and you'll learn how to be a man under my teaching. Someday you may even be able to buy your freedom. By the way, what's your name? I should call you by your name." "My name is Selassie, lord." "That isn't an Arabic name. I'll give you an Arabic name meaning the same thing. What does your name mean?"

"*Selassie* means "Trinity" in my language, lord."

"Trinity! Then you are not a Muslim but a Christian!"

"True, lord. I am from the kingdom of Axum in Ethiopia. We are a Christian people."

I was dumbfounded. I had purchased a Christian slave and was going to Mecca on pilgrimage. Christians are not allowed in Mecca, upon pain of death.

"You'll have to become a Muslim, Selassie. I can't have a Christian slave. I'm going to Mecca; I can't take a Christian there."

Selassie swallowed hard before replying. "With all respect, my lord, I am a Christian, and I must remain a Christian."

I flew into a rage. "Do you dare to defy me? I'll throw you overboard right now if you don't agree to become a Muslim!"

Selassie sat hunched over, his head between his knees, for a long time. His body trembled slightly as he thought about the frightening prospect ahead. Then he rose and bowed low before me. When he spoke, his voice was steady.

"My lord, the Bible, God's Word, says we ought to obey God rather than men. I will obey you in all things except in denying my Savior. I believe you are a kind and just man. Do to me as you will."

In hot wrath, I snatched the boy up and held him by the ankles over the ship's rail, where he could look down at the dark, angry waves sloshing back and forth just a few feet beneath him. I expected him to cry out in fear and beg for mercy, but he did nothing of the sort. He remained silent, his face a picture of peace. I was amazed. I set him down on the deck and began to pace back and forth. I couldn't throw him into the sea; I just couldn't. But what would I do?

Finally, I spoke: "God is merciful, Selassie, and I will be merciful too. But I can't take you to Mecca. I'll have to sell you when we reach Jeddah. We'll be there in ten days. Till then, you will serve me as I command."

I didn't know then, in the silver moonlight of that quiet evening, that we would not reach Jeddah in a fortnight, nor in a month, nor ever.

Chapter 3
The Albatross

As the rising sun began to gild the surface of the dark sea, before I had breakfasted or prayed, the captain approached me with the helmsman at his side. Both men were agitated.

"Sir," he began, "the helmsman brings me disturbing news. He reports that while he was at the wheel last night, he heard you talking with your slave. He's not an eavesdropper, you understand, but you were no more than fifteen feet from him, and he couldn't help overhear you. My man reports that your slave is a . . . a Christian!"

The helmsman, a grizzled old seadog, nodded his head vigorous. "Sir, I will not have an infidel on my ship! You should have dropped him over the side, as you seemed ready to do last night. Why did you hesitate?"

"Captain," I replied soothingly, "Allah is compassionate toward the ignorant, and we must be compassionate too. I will sell him as soon as we reach Jeddah."

"No! That won't do! My man says your miserable slave refused to become a Muslim when given the choice. He has chosen death for himself, and he must die!"

"Captain, surely I don't have to remind you that the boy is my property. By law, I alone have the right to put him to death. I choose to be merciful, as Allah is merciful." The captain spluttered, turned on his heel, and stormed away to his cabin.

Selassie had prudently remained out of sight while the captain and I were exchanging words. When I was alone, he appeared with my breakfast.

"I am sorry I am a source of trouble for you, lord," he murmured as he poured coffee.

"Don't worry, boy. The captain's not a religious man. He doesn't care about the state of your soul, or his own for that matter. He is a superstitious man. He fears Allah may be displeased that he's harboring a Christian aboard his ship and that Allah will strike the ship in wrath. In my opinion, as long as the sky is clear and the weather fair, our captain won't push the matter further."

How wrong I was! In less than an hour, the captain returned to face me again. I wasn't afraid of him, for he was a coward at heart, and I knew I could make him back down. But this time, he brought the entire crew with him. Facing all of them down was a different story. I stood on one side of the deck, placing Selassie behind me; the captain faced me from the other side, the crew lined up behind him.

"Sir," the captain began, "my men and I insist that you throw your slave overboard."

"Captain, you know the law," I replied. "Only the owner has the power of death over his slave when no officer of the Caliph is present. I refuse to sentence my slave to death. And you had better not get any ideas of taking the situation into your own hands. I will not hesitate to report any hostile actions toward my slave to the proper authorities when we reach Jeddah. My slave is worth thirty gold sequins, and I will not allow my property to be harmed."

"We have considered that matter, sir. Thirty gold sequins, you say? Here you are, thirty-five gold sequins." With those words, the captain thrust a bag of coins into my hand while two of the seamen seized Selassie and pulled him over to their side of the deck.

"We have just purchased this little satan, this adversary of the truth. You have even made a profit of five sequins. Now we will deal with him as an enemy of the faith. Let the sea swallow him up!"

"Wait!" I cried desperately. "Don't raise your own hands to slay the lad. I'm returning these thirty-five sequins to you. With them, I am purchasing the ship's dinghy. Put the boy in the dinghy and let him down into the sea. If Allah wants to slay him, he can overturn the boat with a wave or send a great fish to devour him. Allah may choose to be merciful, or he may choose to exercise his wrath. Let that be his decision, not yours."

"That's a good idea, Captain," said one of the seamen. "We'll be rid of the Christian. He won't bring bad luck on us, and we'll still have our thirty-five gold sequins."

"What do you say?" I asked the captain, smiling my broadest, friendliest smile. "You know I don't want to share the deck with a Christian any more than you do, but the Koran doesn't permit us to kill Christians who do us no harm."

"All right," the captain agreed, "That's what we'll do."

The men put Selassie in the dinghy. I insisted that they give him a jug of water, a loaf of bread, and some figs. The men grudgingly gave him these few supplies and then lowered the dinghy into the sea. As the little boat drifted away, Selassie spoke to me for what I thought was the last time.

"Goodbye, lord. Thank you for pleading my cause with the captain. I pray that God takes as good care of you as I trust he will of me."

I watched the little boat till the current bore it out of sight. Stupid, superstitious seamen! I was angry, and sad too, as I watched the boy and the little boat drift away. I had known Selassie only a day, but I had grown fond of him. He did not act at all as I had been led to believe

Christians acted. He seemed to bear no ill will toward me or even toward the captain and crew who cast him adrift. More surprising, twice now, he had faced death with a peace I would not have felt if I had been in his shoes. Well, maybe Allah would choose to preserve his life somehow. I had done all I could. It was time to forget that boy, a boy I hardly knew, and think more about my pilgrimage.

As I turned away from the rail, the captain came up and put his arm around my shoulder.

"I know you think we acted badly toward you, but the helmsman blabbed his tale to the crew, and I had no choice. My crew are simple, untaught men whose heads have been filled with legends and fears in a thousand waterfront cafés. So many things are sure signs of bad luck to them. Discovering a Christian on board is very nearly the worst. Here, I am returning your thirty-five gold sequins. Please don't think I'm a dishonest man."

I took my money and thanked the captain, assuring him that I understood his position and bore no ill will toward him or the crew. Indeed, knowing they were ignorant, superstitious men cooled my indignation. I put thoughts of Selassie out of my mind and turned my eyes to the sea. As my gaze took in the green waters of the Indian Ocean, I began to think again of my pilgrimage. I was nearly halfway to the Red Sea now! For the next three hours, I let my imagination run free. I closed my eyes and pictured what it would be like to visit the holiest places of our religion. How pleasing that would be to Allah!

At noon the crew spread their prayer rugs on the deck, as they did every day. I joined them. In the middle of my devotions, a restless murmur from the other worshippers caused me to lift my head and look around. The men were pointing at the deck and talking in low, agitated tones. No wonder they were disturbed: the shadow of a cross, the hated Christian cross, stretched out on the planks from stem to stern and from one side to the other. We all turned our faces upward, expecting to see some freak cloud, but the sky was empty of all but the ever-burning sun. Shaking their heads in puzzlement, the crew slowly dispersed to their duty stations.

At two o'clock, I made ready to say my afternoon prayers. I glanced up at the sky. It was cloudless, just as it had been for three weeks. As I made ready to kneel down on my prayer rug, a shadow fell over the deck. Even before I looked up, the uneasy muttering of the crew told me that the shadow was once more that of a cross.

This time the crew's alarm could not be calmed. Already they were arguing about the meaning of the cross. Was Allah angry with them because they had cast Selassie into the sea instead of killing him outright? Maybe Allah was angry with that rich man, Sinbad, who argued for the Christian's life. No one suggested that Allah might be angry with them because they had sent an innocent boy to certain death just because he was a Christian, but the thought occurred to me. I remained silent, however, since some of the talk was blaming me.

I looked up. The tropical sky was as empty as ever, but as I scrutinized the face of the heavens, I saw a black spot on the surface of the sun. I took the helmsman's telescope, covered the lens with a silk handkerchief, and squinted at the solar disk through the cloth and the glass. So that was it! The mystery was solved! The black spot was a seabird hovering high between sun and ship, creating the shadow that the crew took as an omen of Allah's wrath. Well, I would take care of that right away!

I went into the captain's cabin and returned with a bow and arrow from the weapons chest. I laid an arrow on the string, arched my body till I was looking straight up at the sun, and drew the arrow back as far as I could. I released the arrow as the puzzled crew looked on, wondering what I was shooting at. Up the arrow flew, up till I could see it no more. Then a faint cry came from on high, the cry of a mortally wounded creature. Within seconds the whole crew could see the bird falling out of the sun, plummeting straight down toward the ship. The bird landed on the deck with a thud, and the men rushed forward to examine its limp carcass.

"There, you see, the cross was not a sign of God's ire. It was only the shadow of a gull or booby, which I've now brought down from the sky. I hope I've relieved everyone's concern."

The captain, who had been bending over the bird, rose to his feet and looked at me. His face, drained of color, looked like a garish death mask in the harsh sunlight.

"Relieved our concern? Proud fool, you have brought certain doom on us. You have done the one thing worse than bringing a Christian on board the ship. You have shot an albatross!"

Chapter 4
The Tempest

The crew shrank back from me as from a loathsome, unclean thing. Fear whelmed up in my heart, for I, too, believed that killing an albatross was a sure sign of coming catastrophe.

"I didn't know; I couldn't know," I babbled. The captain cut me off:

"We'll return to Muscat at once and put this Jonah off the ship before something terrible happens. Helmsman, turn the ship to the northeast. The rest of you, lay on all the sail we have!"

The crew went to work with a will, hurrying past me without a glance or a word. By pretending I wasn't there, they vainly hoped to suppress the terror that gripped them.

Our bad luck began before the helmsman could bring the ship around. The wind that had blown steadily for three weeks died as quickly as the sun vanishes at close of day. We found ourselves becalmed. Our sails hung limp, the tackle hanging down. The ship bobbed gently up and down, going nowhere.

Surrounded by the still, muggy air, with the midday sun glaring down from above and reflecting up from the flat, watery mirror below, the dhow quickly became an unbearable furnace. The men gathered in the stern, surrounding their captain. The rumble of voices and the waving, pointing arms told me I was in for trouble well before the mob lurched toward me.

The captain marched at their head, pushed along more than leading. He stopped before me and spoke in a strained voice:

"Wretch, what calamity your careless act has brought upon our heads!"

"You speak too hastily," I replied, seeking to soothe them. "The wind is only changing direction. See that little cloud, no bigger than a man's hand, there in the south where the sea meets the sky? Before evening a tropical breeze will freshen, and you'll sail before the wind straight back to Muscat."

"Fool, being becalmed is the lightest part of the curse you've brought upon us. At this moment, Mustafa lies in my cabin, burning with fever. An hour ago, he was as sound and vigorous as you and I; now, his life is slipping away. The plague has fallen on this doomed ship like an avenging angel. By nightfall, not a man will be left alive unless we do something with you right away. There's only one thing to do. May Allah have mercy on your soul."

The captain stepped aside, and the men rushed forward. Many hands lifted me from the deck, bore me to the side of the ship, and heaved me over the side into the sea.

The warm ocean closed quickly over me. The depths beneath pulled as with greedy hands on the bag of golden sequins at my belt, dragging me down into the gloom. Seaweed wrapped around my body. Desperately I struggled to unsheathe my knife. When I got it free, I slashed my belt and let the ocean claim the heavy purse. I hacked away the entwining kelp and squirmed out of my robes. Free at last and kicking for my life, I drove my body up toward light and air.

My head broke through the glassy surface just when I thought I could hold my breath no longer. Flailing about and gasping for air, I looked around for the ship. There it was! I cried aloud but knew even as I continued to shout that the crew couldn't hear me. I couldn't have been underwater for more than a minute, but the wind must have risen as soon as I hit the water. With billowing sail, the dhow glided toward the horizon, growing small and vanishing even as I looked after it in helpless despair.

I had been here too many times before, treading water in the open ocean. But on my other voyages, I'd always found a piece of wreckage to climb on or spied a nearby island or hailed a passing merchantman. Now I was floating practically naked in the middle of an empty sea.

"Why, Allah?" I asked in despair. "Why are you so angry with me? I left Baghdad only to fulfill my spiritual duty. But you are not pleased. What can I do to please you so that you will save me? I'll do anything you command if you will save me from an ocean grave."

A voice answered me, but it was not the voice of Allah.

"Swim over this way, lord."

I turned toward the voice. It was Selassie in the dinghy, not ten feet away! I splashed my way over to him and pulled myself into the little boat, then collapsed face down on the bottom, exhausted from my battle with the sea.

"God has been merciful to you, lord, as I prayed. I'm so glad! Here is water and food. And cover yourself with this head cloth so the sun doesn't bake your brain."

I ate and drank but handed the head cloth back to Selassie.

"You need to protect your own head, lad."

"My lord, you are pale, but I am black. God himself has given me protection from the sun."

I put the head cloth on and sat thinking for a while as the dinghy rose and fell with the gentle swell. Then I spoke to the boy who had saved my life.

"Selassie, the crew bought you from me and then cast you away. You're no one's slave now; you're free. You don't need to call me lord anymore. Call me Sinbad, as other free men do."

Selassie's face lit up as he grasped my meaning. "That's true, I'm free! I was born free, I grew up free, and now I'm free again! Praise God! He answered my prayers!

"But I don't think I can call you Sinbad. I was taught to address adults as sir or madam. I'll call you sir until I'm a man; then, I'll call you Sinbad."

"Selassie, that would be fine if we were in Baghdad or Ethiopia, but we're just the two of us in this endless ocean, with very little water and food and no sail or oars. It looks like we won't live long enough for you to grow to manhood unless it pleases Allah to save us in some miraculous way. It seems that we're members in a limited partnership, limited to a few days. We should speak to one another as partners, as equals. You call me Sinbad; I'll call you Selassie."

Selassie smiled. "Very well, Sinbad, we're partners. We'll each contribute what we can to the partnership. You purchased the dinghy. Without it, we would both be dead now. That was your first contribution. I have nothing to contribute, but I'm going to pray to God and ask him to help us. He will be the third partner in our enterprise."

"Well, I hope he'll find you more worthy of reward than he's found me to be," I replied wryly. "But you're not even a Muslim. What have you done to merit his favor?"

"Nothing, Sinbad, nothing at all. But in the Bible, God reveals himself as a gracious God. He is good to the undeserving out of his loving heart. He even sent his Son to die for the sins of the undeserving."

I cut him off before he could say more. "Please; enough of that!

The Koran says God has no son, and I don't want to hear it. Pray if you will, but don't preach to me."

Selassie lifted his hands to heaven and prayed aloud in his own language. I didn't know what he could possibly pray for. Maybe he asked his God to send a ship our way. That's what I would have prayed for, but I felt that Allah was displeased with me and would not have answered any prayer of mine.

Selassie finished praying. We sat silently, looking out at the quiet ocean. By now, the warm air had quite dried me off; indeed, I began to get drowsy as the sun began its slow slide toward the west. I settled my body as comfortably as possible on the hard floorboards and closed my eyes.

When I awoke, it was already dark. I looked up, searching for familiar stars. The dark sky was blank. I sat bolt upright and shook Selassie, who was also sleeping.

"Selassie! Wake up! The sky is overcast; I can't see the stars. I think bad weather may soon be upon us."

I had not finished speaking when a flash of lightning lit up sky and sea. That moment of brightness revealed heavy black clouds scudding along above us. The thunderclap that followed exploded over our heads just as a wall of wind-driven rain hit like a desert sandstorm. The little boat began to pitch and roll.

"Hold on, Selassie! Our only hope is to stay with the boat. I hope the dhow makes Muscat before this tempest catches up with her. She's way too heavy and rides way too low to ride out a storm like this one."

I should have saved my breath; by now, the wind was howling so fiercely that Selassie couldn't hear a word I was screaming at him, though he was only an arm's length away.

The storm raged all night. God must have answered Selassie's prayer because the dinghy didn't capsize even though she continued to fill with water. Bailing was out of the question while the waves continued to beat into the boat. We could only sit in the bottom of our tub and cling to the thwarts for dear life.

After hours of being beaten by the waves, the dinghy began to disintegrate. It was still pitch black when the angry sea shattered the last planks holding the bow and stern sections together, and the little craft broke in two. Selassie was in the bow; I was in the stern. My head was dizzy, and my thoughts were a jumble, but I remember thinking that I would never see Selassie again.

I passed unnumbered hours clinging numbly to the stern section as the storm rampaged on, then weakened, then finally died. The clouds broke up, and the sun won through. I pinched myself. I was alive. I had survived. But, I reflected bitterly, I was still in the middle of the ocean. Selassie's God had not answered his prayers. He was gone, dead or soon to die. I, too, would surely perish before the next sunrise. Then I lifted my head and saw the island.

Chapter 5

The Prophet of the Sun

I wiped the wet hair away from my eyes and blinked twice. The island was still there, a bright green mountain rising out of the ocean less than a mile away. Clutching the remains of the dinghy's stern, I pointed myself at the island and began kicking. The tide carried me toward the island, but it was still slow going, and my strength began to fail. Just when I thought I could not swim another stroke, I felt sand beneath my feet. I stumbled up on the beach, completely spent. I had enough sense left to crawl above the high tide line. There I collapsed unconscious.

When I awoke, my head was throbbing, and the tropical sun was at its zenith. I staggered to my feet and swayed on unsteady legs as I looked up and down the beach. Nothing to my right or left. In front of me, unbroken forest rolled up from the beach all the way to the top of the mountain.

I decided to walk down the beach rather than plunge into the dense wood. I turned to my left and began trudging along the high tide line. After two hours, I came on a stream flowing to the sea from an opening in the trees. I had not had anything to drink for over a day, and my throat was raw and parched. I knelt down on the water's edge and lapped the cool, refreshing water like a dog.

A well-marked path beside the stream disappeared into the forest. "This path was made by people, not animals," I said to myself. "It's bound to lead me to someone who can help me." I forsook the beach and plunged into the green woods.

The path began to switchback up the mountain as soon as it left the beach. Soon I was breathing hard, then panting, then gasping for air. The way became so steep that I had to help my legs by grabbing branches and pulling myself forward. I refused to rest; I had to reach the end of the path and find its makers.

When it seemed my lungs would burst, all at once the path broke out of the trees and flattened out. I found myself in a gently rolling meadow. My heart leaped with joy to see a herd of white humpbacked Brahmin cattle grazing there. Where there were cattle, there had to be people! I kept on the path until I came to a cluster of thatched huts. Cooking fires smoldered in the center of the compound.

"Salaam!" I shouted, proclaiming "Peace!" in Arabic. No one answered. That was strange: someone should be tending those fires. I knocked at one of the huts; no reply. I stuck my head inside the door. No one was home. I tried the other huts without success. The village was abandoned, yet the fires were still burning. It must have been bustling with people less than an hour earlier.

I stood in the middle of the cooking area, wondering what could have happened. Then my stomach, which had been complaining all day, tightened up with pangs that could not be ignored. After all, I hadn't eaten for a day. I lifted the lid off the nearest pot and smelled a delicious curry. Well, supper was ready, but no one had come to the table. It was discourteous to slight the cook! I would do my best to show her, whoever she was, that her work was appreciated. I dished myself up a full bowl and devoured it with gusto, then helped myself to another.

"Thank you, whoever you are, most excellent cook!" I said to no one in particular.

"Oh, you are very welcome," squeaked a voice from behind me, scaring me out of my skin. I whirled round to see a dried-up old man in a white robe grinning at me. The speaker's wrinkled mouth had only four or five yellow teeth left. Spittle dribbled down his chin. He had little hair on his scalp, but a sparse salt-and-pepper beard clung precariously to his chin. His nose was thin, sharp, and curved like the blade of the executioner's sword. His skin was pale and pink. What a repulsive creature!

"I do appreciate your cooking," I managed to say despite his disgusting appearance. "But you've cooked enough food for a whole village, yet no one is here except you and me."

"Oh, I'm not the cook," he replied, "but I bid you welcome on behalf of the women who prepared this meal. They would welcome you warmly if they were here. They ran off with the rest of the villagers when they saw me coming."

"Surely they're not afraid of you," I said. "You are only one, and they must be fifty or more, to judge from the number of huts. Who are you, sir, and why do the villagers hide themselves from you?"

"I am the Prophet of the Sun," the old man replied. "I am a native of this village, but I live apart now. The sun is our god, and I am its prophet. The villagers fear me because they think I am mad. A prophet is without honor in his own country, you know."

So the people of the village were *kafirs*, pagans. They didn't know that the sun was a created thing, made by the one true God. Still, despite their ignorance of Allah, they did have enough sense to know that the old man was a lunatic. Imagine—someone like him claiming to be a prophet!

"Are there any other people on this island?" I inquired.

"Oh yes, I have some followers who also left the village. We live higher up, in a monastery on top of the mountain. Come with me, and you shall have food and shelter. We have another guest, newly arrived today, but there is plenty for all. He was washed up on the beach more dead than alive, but my followers found him and brought him to me. Tomorrow I will send you both to a better place."

Could that rescued guest be Selassie? I wondered. No, that was impossible. But food, shelter, and the promise of a better place sounded good to me. I followed the old man as he turned his back on the village and headed back up the meadow. Glancing back at the village, I was surprised to see a dozen men, dressed in white robes like the prophet, following on my heels.

"Who are these?" I asked the old man.

"They are my choicest disciples. Whenever I visit the village, I take them with me."

"Pardon me for saying so, but they would frighten anybody to look at them. They look more like thugs or goons than disciples of a prophet."

The prophet began to cackle, and his disciples chuckled and cast knowing glances at each other. Soon they were all laughing without restraint.

"Why are you laughing?" I asked, puzzled.

The old man was barely able to stop laughing long enough to speak. "When we reach the monastery, I'll explain why we couldn't keep from laughing at your innocent remark. For now, let me just say that the villagers fear us because they don't accept my prophetic word."

We reached the monastery in less than an hour. It looked more like a fortress than a monastery where men contemplate God in peace. A wall of pointed palisades surrounded the whole place. More men in white robes, armed with spears and bows, stood guard around the monastery.

We passed through the gate into a grassy courtyard. A low building with many doors but no windows ran around the inside wall. The courtyard was empty except for a square block of stone about three feet high lying in its exact center. A long, wavy knife lay on the stone. Clearly, this was the place where the madman and his followers sacrificed animals to the sun.

The prophet led me across the lawn to a door on the far side. "Come in and meet our other guest," he said. The building was dark, and for a while, I could see nothing. As my eyes grew accustomed to the dim light, I saw two large men. Between them was a slender form I recognized at once.

"Selassie, you survived the storm and the sea! Thanks be to Allah! We're out of danger now. This, uh, prophet says he'll send us on our way to a better place tomorrow."

Selassie ran forward and embraced me. As he did, he whispered in my ear: "When you hear this crazy man's plan, you won't be so happy about tomorrow."

"Ah, so you two know each other," the old man said, smiling. "How fitting that tomorrow you will travel together to a better place."

"Tell me about this better place, sir, and how we will get there. Is it a town on this island? Is it another island? India?"

"I suppose now is as good a time as any to explain everything to you, especially since your little friend already knows. I told you that I am the Prophet of the Sun. I didn't tell you that I am also the Priest of the Sun. The sun has revealed to me that I must sacrifice a victim at high noon on the first day of every month or it will become angry and refuse to shine. This afternoon, my disciples and I were going to the village to obtain a victim. Unfortunately, the ignorant, unbelieving villagers aren't eager to offer their lives to their god. I've promised them that willing victims go to spend eternity with the sun, but every month we have to drag one back screaming and fighting. That's why I bring my biggest, strongest disciples with me, the men you called thugs and goons.

"But today, two victims walked right up to us, the boy and you. I hope you believe in me and go joyfully to your death. If you do, you will find bliss in the sun's realm. If you remain an unbeliever, you will die and go into darkness."

The man's speech left me open-mouthed and wordless with astonishment. After seven voyages filled with so many perilous dangers and narrow escapes, a madman with a knife in his hand would be the death of me. How ironic!

"Sinbad," Selassie whispered as the lunatic raved on, "can't you think of some scheme to foil this madman's plan?"

I tried to think, but nothing happened. I'd been in many tough places before, but none like this. I had to play for some time.

I turned to the prophet. "Sir, this is all new to us. We admit that we don't believe in you now, but we invite you to try to convince us that you are the Prophet of the Sun before you sacrifice us. You do want believing victims, don't you? We're too tired now to hear your arguments. Could we talk in the morning, out on the sacrificial stone, before the noon sacrifice?"

"Of course, of course!" the old man agreed eagerly. "You'll see; then you'll go willingly to your death." Turning to his disciples, he gave them orders to lock us up in one of the empty monks' cells.

As the guards led us across the courtyard to our quarters, I whispered to Selassie, "We've got our work cut out for us."

"Or we'll get our hearts cut out of us," quipped Selassie.

"How can you joke at a time like this?" I asked, my anxiety growing by the minute.

"First of all, I know that I have eternal life, no matter what happens tomorrow. The Bible tells us we can know that we have eternal life. Does the Koran make that promise?"

"No, no one can be sure his deeds are good enough to satisfy Allah on the Day of Judgment. That's why I'm afraid, not to mention the thought of that fanatic carving me up with his knife. Did you see the size of that thing?"

"Yes, but I'm confident you'll come up with a plan to save us. Even in Ethiopia, we all knew of that clever man named Sinbad, who cheated death a dozen times."

As Selassie continued to speak of his confidence in God and in me, a faint hope began to flicker in my breast. A plan was forming. Though our chances were slim, the old man was crazy enough that my plan just might work. But it would take all our skill and the favor of Allah.

Chapter 6

The Merciless Sun

The guards shoved us into our room and locked the door. As soon as they left, I told Selassie my plan. He broke into a smile after I explained it. "Perfect, Sinbad! I'll do my part. As you can see by looking at me, God has gifted me for the role you have assigned."

The guards returned in an hour with the evening meal. We had scarcely finished eating before the room began to grow dark. The tropical night was falling fast. Selassie got down on his knees, prayed for a few minutes in his own tongue, and lay down on the rude bed provided. In less than a minute, he was sleeping peacefully. I prayed for a long time, too, but I went to bed just as anxious as I'd been when I sank to my knees. I stretched out on my back, put my hands behind my head, and thought out my plan again and again.

The day dawned bright and clear. I hadn't slept a wink. Selassie was still dozing when the guards came to escort us to the altar of sacrifice. How he had been able to sleep, I couldn't imagine. The boy obviously didn't appreciate the grave danger we faced. Surely there could be no other reason for the calm with which he bade me goodnight after saying his prayers. Did Selassie believe he was so good that his God would somehow save him? Perhaps he had a lot more confidence in my plan than I did.

The guards gave us white robes to wear and led us into the courtyard. It was an hour before noon, the hour of our sacrifice. Already the sun burned down brightly on our heads. The prophet stood waiting at the great, bloodstained stone. It was now or never.

"Here we are, sir, soon to die under your knife. But unless you can convince us that you really are the Prophet of the Sun, we will die unbelievers. Tell us: Why should we believe that the sun is a god or that it chose you to be its prophet?"

"Why should you believe? Because if you don't, you will receive a great chastisement of fire when you die and go to stand before the sun."

"But sir," I replied, "Muhammad said the same thing. He said that men who don't believe he is Allah's messenger would suffer eternal punishment. What proof do you offer us that the sun is really a god and that you are really a prophet?"

"Proof? Why, I have received great revelations from the sun."

"But don't you see, sir, that you only offer us claims, not proof that those claims are true?"

The lunatic began to shake, and sweat broke out on his bald crown. Whether the hot sun or my pigheadedness bothered him more, I couldn't say.

"Confound you, I don't need to give you any proof. Believe or perish!"

"Sir," I continued smoothly, "we stand ready to believe on the basis of evidence. Simply offer us evidence. Can you point to fulfilled prophecies? Miracles?"

"You are so stubborn that I shall not talk with you any further!" he cried. By now, his face was flushed, and sweat was running down his head and neck and soaking his robe. The sun had reached high noon, and its tropical rays hammered our heads with unbearable intensity. The prophet's pale pink skin was turning bright red. I sat down in the shade of the sacrificial stone; it was Selassie's turn now.

Selassie jumped up and began to speak. "My friend Sinbad is too old and set in his ways to change his mind, sir. I am young and may be more open to your persuasion. Tell me why I should accept the sun as my god and you as its prophet."

The mad prophet began once again, reciting the same arguments. Selassie listened politely and responded with soothing words. We had to keep the man standing out in the scorching sun. My friend played his part to perfection, not angering the prophet but keeping him talking.

After an hour, the prophet was swaying back and forth unsteadily on his feet. "Enough, unbelievers! I need to sit down in the shade for a while. I'm feeling faint."

It was time for Selassie to make his move. My friend cried out, "How can you call yourself the Prophet of the Sun and flee from it to embrace the darkness? If the sun has really chosen you as its spokesman, you should be able to bear its friendly rays. I'm only a boy, and I don't believe that the sun is a god. I challenge you: if you don't stay in the sun as long as I do, you're a fake! If I can stand its rays better than you, it will prove to your followers that you're not a real prophet."

The madman looked around the courtyard with glazed eyes. His disciples watched silently from the shade. Even his sunbaked brain knew that his standing with them was on the line. On one side of the stone, bareheaded and smiling, was Selassie. His ebony skin gleamed in the sun. The prophet stood swaying on the other side. His bare head was blistered, peeling, and scarlet as a boiled lobster. The prophet's face twisted in pain as the sun continued to beat down mercilessly on his addled head.

The contest didn't last long. The sun-struck old man clapped his hands over his head and began to stagger around blindly. He fell to his knees babbling, then collapsed face down on the altar. The sun had conquered its would-be prophet.

His followers rushed out to their limp leader. Four of them silently lifted him up and carried him into the nearest building. While they brought water to bathe their fallen idol, Selassie and I quietly stole out of the compound. Once outside, we took off running down the meadow and didn't stop till we reached the safety of the forest.

"Well, my friend, you were right. The black skin Allah gave you was a wonderful gift as you stood in the sun with that crazy man."

"And God gave you the gift of coming up with a clever plan,

Sinbad. Truly, he is gracious to us, though we don't deserve the least of his mercies."

We both knelt down and gave thanks. I recited prayers I had memorized as a child and repeatedly said for years, tried and true prayers from our tradition.

Selassie's prayer was different. I could tell that he wasn't using a formula. He prayed as though he was conversing with his father. How impertinent to be that familiar with God! When we finished giving thanks, we rose to our feet and continued down the path we had trudged up the day before. We would go back to the beach and see if we could find civilized people elsewhere on the island.

We talked as we made our way down to the beach. "Sinbad, the words you spoke to that false prophet raise a question in my mind. How do you know that Muhammad is a real prophet of God? What proof did he provide that his claim to be a prophet was true?"

"What an impertinent question, Selassie! We Muslims know Muhammad is the prophet of Allah because he received the Koran."

"But, Sinbad, as I understand it, the Koran simply states that Muhammad is Allah's messenger and that unbelievers will receive eternal punishment. You said that yourself. But I ask you the question you asked that madman: What is the proof that his claim is true? Did any of his prophecies come true? Did he do miracles and signs?"

"Muhammad prophesied he would return to Mecca after he was forced to flee, and he did. As for miracles, well, Muhammad did none of those."

"Please don't take offense, Sinbad, but Muhammad returned to Mecca at the head of a host of warriors. He fulfilled his own prophecy through human effort. We Christians can point to many prophecies in the Bible that God fulfilled. No man could have made them come true."

"Such as?" I challenged.

"Well," Selassie answered, "the most important prophecy was that God would raise Jesus from the dead after three days and nights in the tomb. Jesus was put to death on a cross and buried in a tomb sealed with a large stone and guarded by Roman soldiers. Three days later, some of his disciples came to the tomb and found the stone rolled away. The tomb was empty. Later that day, they saw Jesus alive again. He certainly didn't rise from the dead by human power. His death and resurrection were prophesied hundreds of years earlier in the sacred Scriptures."

In reply, I explained our belief about Jesus. "We Muslims believe Jesus was a prophet, but we don't believe Allah let him die. We believe Allah substituted a wicked man to die in his place and hid Jesus somewhere. He will come back before the great Day of Judgment."

Selassie responded with a question: "Do you believe a substitute would have fooled the Jewish priests and Romans who put him to death? They knew Jesus; they knew they had executed the right man. If the substitute looked so much like Jesus that he could fool the priests and Romans, they surely would have produced that man's body to stop the rumors that Jesus had risen from the dead. But they didn't, because the tomb really was empty. Truly, Jesus died and then rose from the dead."

Anger and frustration boiled up in my heart. I racked my brain for a withering reply, but nothing came to me. We continued down the path in silence.

I grudgingly admitted to myself that Selassie made some good points. The fulfillment of Muhammad's only prophecy could be explained in purely human terms. Muhammad worked no miraculous signs to prove himself. And it did seem odd that the Jews and the Romans could be fooled by a substitute. Well, there had to be some answer to these perplexities. Selassie was only a boy; surely he couldn't be right and all the scholars of Islam wrong.

Ah, I had it! Islam had conquered its enemies by the power of the sword. Wasn't that proof that Muhammad was the prophet of Allah? The armies of the Caliph had continued Muhammad's conquests, defeating Christian kings and princes. Allah gave us victory over our enemies. Wasn't that proof enough, without miracles? I resolved to put that idea before my Christian companion. But something deep inside me was not satisfied with my own reasoning, and I remained silent for the present.

Chapter 7
Danger Under the Waves

We reached the beach by late afternoon. "Well, which way do you want to go, to the right or to the left?" I asked.

"Use your own judgment, Sinbad. This is my first shipwreck; you're the one with experience," Selassie joked. I could see that escaping from the mad prophet had put the lad in a carefree mood.

"We'll go to the right. That way, the sun won't be in our eyes," I declared. That wasn't much of a reason, but there was no better reason for choosing one direction over the other. We began trudging north, with the sun on our left. At dusk, we left the beach for the trees to find a hiding place where we could sleep without being seen. Perhaps the prophet's goons were following us; I didn't want to take any chances. We shoved our way into a thicket of tropical shrubs and found a patch of grass in the center. We collapsed on the ground and fell asleep instantly. It had been an exhausting day.

Our growling stomachs roused us well before sunrise. We hadn't eaten in over a day. Shaking the sleep from our heads, we walked down to the beach and pushed on, plodding through the sand in hopes of finding another human being, or at least a coconut palm, where we could satisfy our hunger. Our efforts were rewarded before noon when we spied a cluster of tiny figures far up the beach. Quickening our pace, we soon came upon them. They proved to be a group of pearl fishers. To my delight, they spoke Arabic.

"Peace be upon you, brothers," I greeted them in traditional fashion.

"And upon you, lord," they replied. I asked them where they lived. They answered that they were from Zanzibar. And why were they here? Why, to dive for pearls! They informed me that this island was well known to the pearl fishers of Zanzibar. Every year they undertook a hazardous six-week voyage here to dive for the largest pearls to be found anywhere in the Indian Ocean.

"It is very dangerous, lord. Why, we have been here only a week, and already we have lost a dozen men. Every year barely half of us return."

"Were your companions carried off by the Prophet of the Sun?" I asked. They looked puzzled, so I told them of our encounter with the madman who almost took our lives. They told me they had never heard of him.

"No, lord, the danger doesn't come from the island. It lurks under the waves. Monsters on the ocean bottom guard the oysters that grow the pearls! If a man can gather the oysters and return safely to the boats, he will be wealthy. But too many men with high hopes dive beneath the waves, never to see the sun, their friends, or their families again."

"Surely it can't be worth the risk!" I exclaimed. In answer, the leader of the group opened the basket at his feet and handed me a heavy lump wrapped in a turban.

"See for yourself," he said. I unwound the turban to expose a pearl the size of a goose egg! It was perfectly round and shone from within with a creamy white light. I had bought and sold many pearls on my seven voyages, but never had I seen a pearl like that pearl! Haroun al-Rashid would have given both his summer and winter palaces for such a pearl. For size, form, and color, it was a jewel without price.

"I admit this pearl is larger than most, lord. Most of the pearls are no bigger than grapes or quail eggs. Nor are they all pure white. Some are pink, some yellow, a few glow blue or green. One or two such pearls is all it takes to make a man wealthy in Zanzibar. Can you see now why we are willing to risk our very lives?"

I nodded and stood gazing dumbly at the pearl. I couldn't take my eyes off it. The leader of the group wound the turban around his treasure again and returned it to the basket. Only with the pearl out of sight could I think clearly.

"I must fish for pearls too!" I exclaimed.

"Sinbad," Selassie broke in, "we want to get off this island and back to the mainland as soon as possible. You can't stay here and defy death by diving into a pool of monsters."

I ignored Selassie as I questioned the leader. "You've lost a dozen men already. You could use a skilled seaman. Take my friend and me back with you. I know the sea like the back of my hand. The boy's no seaman, I admit, but I know from experience that he can cook. Let us join your band."

"We've no objections," the leader replied. "There's plenty of pearls for all, if the monsters don't get you first, and there's plenty of room in our boat now. There's no denying that we could use another hand who knows the sea, and we could certainly use a better cook! Mark you well: we plan to stay only three more days. We must return to Zanzibar before the monsoon breaks."

Selassie could see that my mind was made up, and he didn't continue to object. In fact, he entered into the spirit of the venture by volunteering to begin cooking right away so the men could dive for another hour before prayers and the midday meal. My unhappy stomach reminded me that Selassie was hungry too. Clever scamp! He would get his breakfast now, better late than never!

I stripped down to a loincloth and walked over to join the men at the water's edge. Some had already made several dives and were now sitting in the sand, opening their oysters; others were just wading into the surf.

"How far out are the oyster beds?" I asked one young diver who was busy opening his catch.

"They're about a hundred yards out," he answered. I borrowed a knife from him, tucked it into my loincloth, and plunged into the surf. In waist-deep water, I kicked off and began to swim toward the oyster beds. When I got there, I found a dozen men already at work diving beneath the surface, popping up again to gulp fresh air, and treading water to rest a bit before slipping under the warm waves again. Over and over, they returned to the bottom of the sea till their canvas pouches bulged with flat, gray oysters.

"Well, here goes," I told myself. Filling my lungs till they could hold no more, I dove under the surface and kicked my way to the bottom.

The beds were only fifteen feet down. Tropical sunlight beamed down through the crystal waters and brightened the white sandy seafloor. Colorfully striped and spotted fish glided lazily through spires of yellow, pink, and red coral. Between the coral formations, waving ribbons of yellow and olive seaweed rose from black rocks half-buried in the sand. And yes! Some of those rocks bore oysters instead of seaweed. I cut a clutch of oysters from the nearest rock and kicked my way back to the surface. Time to return to the shore and examine my catch, I thought. My stomach complained that it was also well past the time to eat. My mind knew Selassie would have the midday meal ready by the time I returned, but my stomach continued to object all the way back to the beach.

The men of Zanzibar were Muslims like me, so we all assembled on the beach for prayers before opening up our prizes. We hurried through prayers and quickly fell to prying the shells apart. No one wanted to eat till he had examined his catch: greed was stronger than hunger.

What a scene it was! One man would shout with joy when he found a pearl, and another would curse or sigh to find he had risked his life for shells that held only quivering oyster meat. One after another, my oysters proved empty until I popped the top off the last one and saw a silky pink pearl lying on a pillow of grayish-white flesh. The pearl was small, the size of a cherry pit, but perfectly formed. It would fetch a pretty sum in Baghdad if I ever managed to return.

Saying nothing to the pearl fishers, I went and told Selassie the news.

"You must join me in diving for pearls, Selassie. We'll need some money to buy passage home from Zanzibar."

"If you say so, Sinbad," he replied without enthusiasm. "I'm not much of a swimmer, and you heard what the men said about monsters."

"I saw no monsters. I don't think there are any. Besides, the water is light and clear down there. Anyone who keeps his eyes open should be able to avoid getting caught. By the way, when do we eat?"

"The chief pearl fisher says we must wait for a man named Omar. He was the last man to go into the water. We'll eat when he returns."

We waited for Omar a long time—too long. Something must have happened to him, the men said, shaking their heads. Two of them swam out to the oyster beds and looked around, diving to the bottom several times. When they returned, their faces told us they had seen no sign of him.

"There's no doubt about it," a man named Ali said. "Omar was carried off by a monster."

"Has any of you actually seen one of these monsters?" I asked.

"No, but what other explanation can there be for the disappearance of one fine diver after another? Our comrades were strong, alert, and armed with knives. Only a giant undersea monster could take them away and leave no trace."

We walked back to the cooking fire, and Selassie dished us up a mouth-watering yellow fish curry heaped on jasmine rice. The savory odor of the curry wafted over the beach, but the men sat in anxious silence and only picked at their food. Each asked himself, Who would be next? They never thought of abandoning their risky work: the thought of becoming rich gripped each man's mind. The idea of giving up the search for pearls never entered my head, either. I was already wealthy, but the greed that never says, "Enough!" was burning in my brain.

Over the next two days, I dove morning and afternoon. By the morning of our departure, I had a pouch stuffed with two dozen pearls. They would be worth at least twenty-five thousand gold sequins. Selassie always excused himself from diving, pleading the need to get the next meal going. But after breakfast on our last day, I insisted he accompany me on my final dive.

"Even one pearl will make you well-to-do in Ethiopia," I said, trying to persuade him.

Selassie thought for a minute. Finally, he agreed: "I'll make one dive. Someday I may have to buy the freedom of my father or some other enslaved countryman. But I don't need any pearls for myself. I already possess a pearl of great price."

"What do you mean? You haven't been diving at all. Where did you get this pearl? I haven't seen it."

Selassie replied, "The Bible says that the kingdom of heaven is like a pearl of great price so valuable that a merchant will sell all he has in order to buy. And yet, we can never pay for it. Jesus paid for it when he died for our sins on the cross. No one else could pay the price of that pearl! Then he gives this priceless pearl to us as a gift! We can do nothing but receive the gift by faith."

"Are you telling me that no man can do enough good to earn paradise?"

"That's right. You're a good Muslim, but you're still concerned that God may not find you good enough. Do you know anyone so good that God is bound to let him into his heaven?"

I didn't answer my friend, for I couldn't think of anyone I was sure would be in paradise. The scholars and imams of Islam knew a lot, but knowledge wouldn't tip Allah's judgment scales in their favor.

"Let's talk about this later when we're not so hurried," I finally replied. "We need to get that last dive in before the ship sails for Zanzibar." The ship would leave before dark, but that still gave us plenty of time.

I gave Selassie a knife, and we walked down to the edge of the sea, where the warm water ran in after each wave and covered our toes. We waded into the waves and swam out to the oyster beds. Selassie proved to be a better swimmer than I expected, and we reached our goal in just a few minutes.

"Keep in sight of me when we're on the bottom," I said. "In case either of us sees anything frightening, he can warn the other." We both took a large gulp of air and dove to the bottom. I looked around and saw coral and seaweed, nothing more. I motioned to Selassie to indicate where the oysters lay, and he nodded his head. We both went to work hacking clumps of oysters loose. Selassie swam back to the beach to open his oysters while I kept diving. Soon he was back in the water. With a big grin, he held up two gleaming pearls for me to admire.

Selassie stuffed the pearls in his belt and immediately dove to the bottom again. I followed him, and we continued to chop away at the masses of oysters clinging to the coral.

When my hands were full, I headed toward the light above. I reached the surface, took a breath of fresh air, and looked around for Selassie. I kept waiting—a half-minute, a full minute. Something was wrong! I dropped my oysters and headed for the bottom again. I soon found my friend and knew why he had not risen to the surface with me. His foot was caught in the jaws of a giant clam!

Chapter 8

The New Order

I had only a minute to free Selassie from the clam, or it would be too late. I drew my knife and thrust it between the massy shells that gripped my friend's ankle, stabbing deep into the clam's soft flesh. The shells held firm. I jabbed my knife again and again, hoping to find the muscles that pulled the shells together. After a dozen blows, a lucky thrust cut one of the muscles, and the clam relaxed its hold. Selassie jerked his foot loose, and we both headed for the surface. I gave Selassie a triumphant thumbs up: we had cheated death again!

I celebrated too soon. Without warning, rubbery arms grabbed me from behind, wrapping around my chest and legs. Other arms shoved a glass bowl filled with air over my head. I gasped, filling my lungs with fresh air. Twisting around to see who had laid hands on me, I found myself face-to-face with a giant octopus! Ten feet away, a second octopus had entwined its tentacles around Selassie and jammed a bowl on his head.

Shooting jets of water out behind them, the octopuses propelled themselves down, down into the depths of the ocean. The light faded to blackness as they bore us into the abyss. Then, to my amazement, I saw a light below. The monsters were making straight for the light.

As we drew near, I saw that the light poured forth from a huge crystal dome rising from the seafloor. The octopuses brought us to a door in the side of the dome, opened the door, and shoved us inside.

We found ourselves in a small room with two doors—an outer door, which we had come through, and an inner door at the back. The room was full of water. After the octopuses had shut the outer door, we heard a sucking sound, and the water level began to drop. As soon as the room was pumped dry, the inner door opened, and a man walked briskly into the room. He wore a light-green turban with a large pearl on the forehead and a dark-green robe made of a fabric I didn't recognize. The man in green stopped in front of us, folded his arms, and looked us up and down. He didn't smile or speak. The brow above his bearded face was furrowed with thought.

After a few anxious minutes, the man addressed us: "You may take the bowls off your heads now and breathe freely. You two don't know how lucky you are that we didn't have the octopuses rip you to pieces and feed your limbs and organs to the sharks. That was the fate of your greedy companions. We've spared you only to satisfy our curiosity. Why didn't you abandon your quest and return home as fast as possible when your companions started to disappear? Why did you continue to take oysters from our private pearl ground even as your men vanished one by one? What kind of men are you who risk your lives for cheap baubles like these?"

As the man spat out the last question, he cast a handful of pearls at our feet. I had to force myself to look at the man and not the pearls as I searched for a reply. I began to stammer, knowing that our lives hung in the balance. Then a story just came to me. It wasn't the truth, but I was afraid to tell the truth.

"We're grateful to be here, sir, wherever we may be, and we're grateful to you, whoever you may be. You see, we were practically the slaves of those pearl fishers. We are castaways. We met up with the pearl fishers only a few days ago. They sailed here from Zanzibar over hundreds of miles of ocean. They promised to take us back to Zanzibar with them if we would gather pearls for them. They are very greedy for pearls. We have no interest in acquiring pearls for ourselves; we seek only to return to our own home."

"I don't believe you," the man in green snapped. "I saw your eyes gleam when I threw those pearls on the ground. You're as greedy as any man under the sun."

Then Selassie spoke up for the first time since our capture. He seemed none the worse for almost drowning and replied with force and vigor. Youth is a wonderful thing, I thought.

"My friend told you truth, sir, though I regret to say that it was not all true. It's true that we are castaways and want to return home more than anything. I confess, though, that my friend is fonder of pearls than he admits. You could see that. My friend is Sinbad the Sailor, a renowned traveler and merchant of Baghdad. Sinbad always wants to turn a profit, even when he's shipwrecked. He hoped to restore his fortunes by finding pearls.

"But Sinbad is a generous man who gives freely of his vast wealth. He's also a kind man, as I can testify from my own experience. He bought me from slavers and later saved my life at risk to his own. Thanks to him, I'm alive and free."

"Sinbad the Sailor! I remember hearing of you years ago when I walked under the sun. Well, Sinbad, because of the honesty of your friend, his testimony of your good character and deeds, and your own reputation, we will spare your lives. But we can't allow you to return to the world above the waves. You'll have to live the rest of your lives here in our city undersea."

"We, you say?" I asked. "How many of you are there? Do you really *live* down here? How did you come here? What do you do? Why can't we leave here?" The questions came tumbling out of my lips, one after another, till the man in green held up his hand to stop me.

"I'll answer all your questions soon enough since you're now part of our community. I am the First Comrade, the leader of the community. Come, let me take you on a tour of the city while we talk."

The First Comrade picked up the pearls he had thrown down and shoved them in his sash. He then opened the inner door and beckoned us to follow him. Passing through the door, we entered the dome itself.

The arched vault was immense, bigger than the Great Mosque of Baghdad. A village of houses and larger buildings, all constructed of coral blocks, occupied most of the seafloor within the dome's glass walls. A water-filled tank as big as one of the houses sat directly under the center of the dome and reached nearly to its top. The tank teemed with glowing worms, large and small fish with luminous spots and stripes, and strange marine creatures that shone with soft green and blue light.

"We call that tank the Pool of Light. It is the source of light for our new world," our guide said.

"New world?"

"Yes. We who live and work here think of ourselves as pioneers of a new human race, the creators of a new and better world. We grew disgusted with the ignorance, fear, hatred, and violence up there under the sun. From many lands, we banded together to make a new beginning for our race. From east to west, the earth is full of corruption, so we decided to build a colony on the bottom of the sea. This is now the Year Ten of the New Order."

I stared in wonder at the soaring vault, the glowing tank, the houses, and the buildings. "No builder on earth possesses enough knowledge to construct a dome like this!" I exclaimed. "Where did you obtain such wisdom?"

"One of our colonists is an Egyptian from the great and ancient city of Alexandria. You may remember that a Muslim army captured

Alexandria and destroyed its great library several hundred years ago. The librarian was able to save a few rare volumes, as many as he could carry in his arms when he fled. He hid them till he was near death and then entrusted them to his son. The son passed them on to his son, and so on down to the present day. The last keeper of the books joined our cause.

"In those books, we found the secret of building the crystal dome, the Pool of Light, and many other marvelous devices. We are building the New Order on an ancient foundation."

"Alexandria was a seat of Christian learning," Selassie broke in. "Do you have a Bible?

"A Bible! We need no Bible. The Bible is for the ignorant and for sinners. We are the cream of the human race in mind and spirit. We are building a new human race without help from any god."

The First Comrade stopped and looked me up and down.

"You must be a Muslim. Muslims destroyed the great library of Alexandria. For that alone, we should have the octopuses tear you limb from limb and feed you to the fishes."

"So much for giving up violence," Selassie whispered to me. The man took no notice of Selassie's remark and went on speaking as we crossed the dome. But his attitude toward us changed when he realized I was a Muslim and Selassie was a Christian.

"I was hasty when I said you could join our colony. I'll have to bring you before the assembly and let it decide if we are to spare your lives." With that, the First Comrade put a coiled seashell to his lips and blew a long, low trumpet blast. Immediately people began to come out of the houses and make for one of the large buildings. By the time we drew near the building, a crowd of men and women was already clustered in front of the door. They eyed us warily as we approached. We entered the building, and all the people filed in behind us.

We found ourselves in a large meeting room. The First Comrade led us to the front of the room and motioned that we should sit in chairs placed in front. The colonists also sat down, facing us. I smiled broadly at them, but none of them returned my smile. When all the inhabitants of the dome were present, their leader stood up and explained why he had called them together.

"Comrades, the man and boy in front of you were captured in the act of raiding the oyster beds. You must decide whether they are to live with us or die. The man is Sinbad the Sailor." At those words a murmur of recognition spread through the assembly. The First Comrade continued: "As for the boy, I don't know his name. What is your name, boy?"

"My name is Selassie, sir."

"Fine. Young Selassie did speak on behalf of Sinbad. He affirmed that Sinbad is a kind man who freed him when he was a slave and later saved his life. You may put that much down in Sinbad's favor. Against him, we have the fact that he was stealing our pearls. He claims to be a castaway and says he wanted pearls only to buy passage home for himself and the boy. That was a lie. The boy confessed that Sinbad wanted pearls to become rich.

"You must decide the fate of these intruders. I've already told them that they will never return to dry land, but it may be your wish to dispose of them now. What say you?"

An older woman rose to speak. "I say we can't take a chance on them. Sinbad is a greedy man, like all the rest of them in the upper world. We are the pure; we don't want any base people here."

"I agree," added a bushy-bearded man. "Besides, two more colonists would be two more mouths to feed and two more partners to share the wealth we're mining here undersea. I want my full share."

"Agreed!" exclaimed another man. "I don't like their looks either."

"I doubt whether they are intelligent enough to join our evening conversations. Their talk would be so, so ordinary and worldly! We discuss philosophy and the arts. What could a common merchant and a mere boy contribute to our dialog?"

The rest of the comments were of the same sort. When the vote was finally taken, the whole assembly, to a man, voted to condemn us to death.

"May I speak to this exalted gathering?" Selassie asked after the First Comrade announced the tally. "Surely noble folk like you can spare me a little time."

With a wave of his hand, the leader permitted Selassie to speak.

"I won't take up much of your time since you would rather be discussing great things," my friend said bitingly, "but I have four questions to ask before we die. First, how can you build a pure society when your hearts are evil? You say you hate ignorance and violence, yet you remain happily ignorant of what we are, while you condemn us to a violent death. Second, why do you believe you can build a noble society based on the wisdom of the ancients? They were proud, cruel, and wicked, just as you propose to be with us! Third, do you really think you can make a better human race without bowing to God, who created the human race? You reject the Bible and have no guide except your own deluded minds. Fourth, how long do you think you can live here without turning on each other? There, I said it, and I'm glad!"

Pandemonium broke out. "Scandalous!" "What impertinence!" "Away with them!" "Not another word!" "Who does that boy think he is?" I was afraid the assembly would turn into a mob and tear us apart. The leader blew his trumpet, and the shouts gradually died out; but I could feel the anger and hate that Selassie's rash words had stirred up. I had to do something, or we were done for. I climbed up on my chair, smiled broadly again, and began to plead with them before their leader could order our execution.

"Please, friends! Hear me, I pray! My companion is only a boy. He's too young to recognize your nobility, a nobility revealed even in your just judgment on us. Yes, I admit that your verdict was fair; but may I ask for mercy? Nobility, wisdom, and purity are displayed most clearly in generosity and mercy toward the undeserving and ignorant. Are your hearts big enough to show mercy to two wretches like us? Mercy would be a glorious testimony to the greatness of your souls."

A man wearing a light-blue turban and a dark-blue robe approached the leader and whispered something to him. After more whispering back and forth, the man in blue spoke to us.

"The First Comrade suspends the judgment of the assembly for ten days while we observe your behavior. Perhaps you will show yourselves worthy of a second trial. Till then, you are free to go wherever you will in the dome. Don't try anything funny. All the people will be watching you and forming their judgments."

Well, I had won us another ten days of life. But could we win over the people and secure a pardon?

Chapter 9
Bloodstones and Treachery

The colonists filed out of the hall, and we were left alone with the man in blue, who informed us he was the Second Comrade.

"I'm sorry I got us into trouble with my speech," Selassie said to me. "What I said was true, but it wasn't very smart. I guess I was casting my pearls before swine."

"What do you mean by that?" I asked.

"The Lord Jesus Christ told us not to cast our pearls before swine. I think he meant that it's no use to give God's truth to the hard-hearted, because they won't value it. I hoped God might use my rebuke to prick their consciences and change their hearts. I should have recognized that he wasn't at work in them, but I'm only a child, and I can't read faces very well, to say nothing of hearts. Still, Sinbad, I sense that God is at work in your heart."

"You mean, you hope your God will persuade me to become a Christian?" I asked scornfully. "There's no chance of that. I am glad you said so, though. If I thought you considered me a swine, our friendship would be over: we Muslims detest pigs!"

The Second Comrade interrupted us. "Enough of that religious talk! It won't impress my comrades and me. Our great leader already told you that we reject all gods and all holy books. You asked him if the Egyptian brought a Bible from Alexandria. Well, he did, but we can't read it—not that we want to, of course. It's not in Greek; it's in the language of Ethiopia, which none of us understands."

Selassie trembled with excitement. "Sir, I'm from Ethiopia! If your Bible is in Geez, our language, I can read it. Since you can't read it and don't want it, could I buy it from you? I have two pearls that I was going to save for an emergency, but I would gladly give them to you for the Bible."

The Second Comrade looked to the left and right. The hall was empty except for the three of us. "Let me see the pearls," he whispered. Selassie took the pearls from his belt and handed them over. The man rolled them around in the palm of his hand, savoring their creamy smoothness with his sweaty fingers and sparkling eyes. Clearly, they pleased him.

"Agreed," he said. "But say nothing to any of the people about this. We share all things in common here, so I will put these pearls in the common purse when, uh, I have the opportunity. Till then, it will be our little secret." He stuffed the pearls in his waistband and gestured for us to follow him.

The Second Comrade led us out of the hall and across the floor of the dome to another large building. We entered and found ourselves in a library. No one else was there. The man opened a drawer in the librarian's desk and pulled out a book bound in black leather embossed with strange gold letters.

"It is a Bible!" Selassie exclaimed. "I can read those letters!" The lad picked up the Bible and opened it reverently. As he looked at the text, his face lit up, and he broke into a wide grin.

"Take it," the Second Comrade said with a tight, thin-lipped smile. I didn't trust that smile. All too soon, I would discover that my mistrust was fully warranted.

Selassie clutched the Bible tightly as the Second Comrade led us out of the library into the great crystal dome again. "I have to check on the mining operations at the far end of the colony," he said. "You may follow me around or wander wherever you want as long as you stay in sight of a comrade." With those words, he turned and left.

"Where should we go, Sinbad?" asked Selassie. Selassie was willing to go wherever I wanted, so we hurried after the blue figure walking briskly ahead of us. Then, suddenly, the Second Comrade vanished from sight, right before our eyes! He had stopped a few feet from the far wall of the dome, and then he was gone! When we reached the place where we saw the man disappear, the mystery was solved. A hole gaped in the ground at our feet. A ladder poked up through a hole. That must be the mine, I thought. The Second Comrade must have gone into the hole. I climbed down the ladder, and Selassie followed.

When we arrived at the bottom of the hole, we found ourselves in a tunnel lighted with bowls of glowing fish like those in the Pool of Light. As we walked down the tunnel, we came upon colonists chipping at the sides of the tunnel with picks and hammers. From time to time, one of the workers would dislodge a sparkling crimson gem, which he would put in a bucket at his feet. Finally, we caught up with our guide.

"Those stones are magnificent!" I exclaimed. "What are they?"

"They are unknown in the land beneath the sun," the Second Comrade replied. "Down here, we call them bloodstones."

"Each one must be worth a fortune!" exclaimed Selassie, eyes bulging at the fiery gems. "What do you do with them?"

"We put them in our treasury."

"But then what? Do you fashion jewelry out of them? Do you use them for money? Do you plan to sell them up on dry land?"

"None of that," the Second Comrade answered. "We recognize their great value, but we haven't been able to agree on what to do with them. None of the courses of action you suggest agrees with our lofty principles. Until we can find a noble use for them, we'll continue to store them."

The Second Comrade walked up and down the tunnel, talking with the colonists laboring at their tasks. Some of the men and women picked at the sides of the tunnel while others dug away at the end of the tunnel, burrowing further into the rock. While the Second Comrade did his work, Selassie and I talked.

"Sinbad, I don't understand these people. They reject as base and unworthy all the uses men have for precious stones, but they continue to dig them out of the seafloor. Why do they heap up jewels they cannot use? Jewels are just so many rocks down here undersea."

"Your guess is as good as mine. Like you, I can't see into the human heart."

"They're no different from people up under the sun," Selassie mused. "So many people, yours and mine, spend their lives getting and hoarding riches they have to leave behind when they pass from this life into eternity. You're a rich man, Sinbad. Why do you put your life in danger again and again by sailing off to faraway lands in search of more wealth? You already have more than you can ever use, even if you should live to be a hundred. Of course, that's not likely now, is it?"

"I haven't got a good answer for you, Selassie. Even before I left Baghdad on this unlucky voyage, I knew I had to devote myself to Allah and not to chasing after more gold and silver. Now it looks like I'll die before I get to Mecca. I hope Allah accepts the good works I've done so far because I'm not going to get the chance to do many more before these wicked people feed us to the fishes. I wish I'd given more away when I was able; instead, I tried to gain more and more."

"When we get some time to ourselves, Sinbad, I want to read you some parts of the Bible that are precious to me. They are just what you need. They tell of how God himself provided for us the good works he requires of us. They were done by Jesus, but they were done for us."

"Yes, yes, that's fine; tell me later. Here comes our rescuer, guide, and judge."

The Second Comrade returned from inspecting the end of the tunnel. "How far does the tunnel extend?" I asked.

"Well, today I walked for ten minutes till I came to the end. Every day our diggers extend it more. We will continue to hammer and pick our way forward till we come to the end of the bloodstones."

"Aren't you afraid you may dig your way through the ocean floor and flood your colony?" Selassie inquired.

"Have you forgotten that we who have chosen to live here are the wisest of the wise?" retorted the Second Comrade with a huff. "We are not gripped by the greed that pushes prudence aside in its mad rush for gain; we know exactly what we are doing. I am slightly insulted by your question."

With that, the Second Comrade turned and started back toward the ladder. We followed him without saying a word. After we climbed out of the hole, we left the Second Comrade and wandered around the dome for several hours, doing nothing. Always we were under the suspicious gaze of the comrades.

At last, one of the miners climbed out of the hole, lifted a conch shell to his lips, and sounded a long blast. The workday was over. The miners emerged from underground caked with a paste of rock flour and sweat and filed into a low building that served as the public bathhouse. About a quarter hour later, the trumpet sounded again, and all the colonists began to make their way toward the third large building. We followed them and found that it was the community's dining hall. We were allowed to eat at a table with the others, but no one spoke to us despite our attempts to make conversation. The trumpet blew again, and everyone stood up at once and trooped out of the building.

The Second Comrade walked over to our table. "In fifteen minutes, the timekeepers will lower a shroud over the Pool of Light to make our night. By then, you must be in bed. I'll take you to the house where you'll sleep."

We rose obediently and followed him to a house at the far end of the dome. The house had but a single room with four beds. Two of the beds were already occupied by colonists—our guards. It became clear that we were to be watched by someone all the time and never left alone. We were too exhausted to care. We tumbled into our beds and instantly fell asleep.

I was dreaming of the world above the waves when I felt a hand shaking me. I opened my eyes to see Selassie with his finger over his lips. He silently beckoned me to follow him. We tiptoed past our snoring guards and slipped out the door. Black drapes covered the Pool of Light, but the dome was not completely dark, and I could follow Selassie without difficulty. We flitted from the shadow of one building to the next until we reached the dining hall. Inside the empty building, we could speak without fear of being caught.

"Sinbad, I have something important to tell you. I couldn't sleep, thinking of my family and everything. I was looking out the window when I saw the First Comrade and the Second Comrade creeping across the dome toward the library building. Something made me get out of bed and follow them. I sneaked into the building after them. Did you know that the library building is also the treasury? I watched those two fine comrades put the largest and most brilliant gems into a bag, which they then carried out of the building. I followed them to a small house next to the airlock where we entered the dome. Do you know what they did then?"

"Tell me."

"They stashed the bag in a large glass ball big enough to hold two men and a lot of treasure. Do you know what I think? I think they plan to forsake the colony when they have stolen enough jewels!"

"You could be right," I agreed. "Do you think they're leaving tonight?"

"No; they both returned to their own houses afterward. I think they steal just a few bloodstones each night so that the guardians of the treasury don't detect the loss. The glass ball isn't nearly as full as it could be."

Selassie led me to the guardhouse, and I peeked in at the glass ball. This could be our escape! But before we could examine the ball, we heard voices over by the Pool of Light. The timekeepers were getting ready to raise the curtain on a new day. We scurried back to our house and climbed into our beds just before light flooded the colony and the community woke up for another day.

After breakfast, Selassie and I went for a walk. As long as we kept moving, we could talk, and no one could listen in on our conversation. We decided to try to escape the next night. Our wanderings took us back to the mine. The Second Comrade was coming up the ladder just as we arrived at the hole. Without as much as a "Good morning," he walked past us toward the house of the First Comrade.

As I watched him walk away, I saw a sight that made my heart drop within me. "Selassie!" I burst out, so loudly that the Second Comrade turned around and frowned at me. I lowered my voice to a whisper and spoke to my friend. "Look at his footprints: they're damp!" Selassie squinted at me, puzzled.

"Don't you see?" I continued. "There must be water seeping into the tunnel. The colonists have dug too far. Sooner or later, the tunnel will give way, and the sea will burst into the tunnel. If that happens, water will gush up into the dome, and everyone will die!"

We chased down the Second Comrade. "Sir, wait!" I cried. The man stopped, and in a few breathless words, I warned him of the disaster looming over the colony. "You must tell the colonists to stop digging at once. One blow too many, and the wall will collapse, and the water will pour in."

"Yes, I see," the Second Comrade said when I paused for breath. "It seems I was overconfident back in the tunnel. But we must not alarm the others." He raised his shell to his lips and blew a blast that brought the miners out of the hole and the rest of the colonists out of their houses. As before, everyone headed for the meeting hall.

The Second Comrade talked quietly with the First Comrade while they waited for the stragglers to arrive. When all were assembled, the First Comrade spoke.

"We're ending work early today. It's time to carry out the community's judgment on these two thieves. I know that I declared we would give them ten days to prove themselves, but they have already behaved unworthily. The boy has stolen a book from the library. It is only a Bible, of no value to us, but the act of stealing it reveals that earth's society has already corrupted him beyond even our power to remedy. Sinbad knew what the boy did but said nothing. I declare that the death sentence voted by the community must be carried out immediately!"

A roar went up from the assembly. I shouted, trying to tell the real story, but I couldn't even hear myself, so deafening was the angry tumult. The leader blew his trumpet, and the colonists fell silent.

"Take them back to their house and set a guard. In exactly one hour, we will thrust them into the airlock and let the water and the octopuses in. You'll all be able to see them torn apart." Another roar went up from the assembly, a roar of approval. The First Comrade selected four brawny miners to escort us back to our house, now a prison for the condemned. As they dragged us away, I tried again to tell the people what had really happened and what great danger they faced, but a guard clapped his hand over my mouth. Before we had time to be afraid, we were marched across the square, pushed into our house, and locked inside.

Chapter 10

Qismat?

"Here we are again, Sinbad, locked in a room and facing death in an hour, just as when we were prisoners of the Prophet of the Sun. Do you have another plan to cheat the executioner?"

"I wish I did," I replied with a grimace. For a few minutes, which seemed like hours, we slumped without speaking in the dim room.

"Why do you think the two comrades decided to kill us now?" asked Selassie, finally breaking the silence.

"My guess is that they don't want us to tell what we know about water leaking into the tunnel. That can only mean they plan to escape secretly as soon as possible. If only there were some way to warn the rest of the colonists, they would forget about killing us and go after their leaders! But the two comrades will never permit us to speak."

"Then we'll let the stones speak for us!" Selassie cried. "Leave it to me, Sinbad; this time, *I* have the plan."

Before my young friend could tell me his scheme, the guards entered the room. They stuffed rags in our mouths so we couldn't talk and marched us off to the airlock, where the people were already elbowing and shoving to get a place right in front of the thick, crystal window. The mood was festive: what fun to watch the octopuses rip our arms and legs off! The colonists wanted to build a new society, but their old human nature had not changed.

The First and Second Comrades approached to pronounce the official decree of doom. But before they could open their mouths, Selassie leaped forward and pulled on the Second Comrade's sash. Out tumbled the pearls the man had taken from Selassie in exchange for the Bible. Then he jerked the First Comrade's sash, and the pearls he had cast at our feet in the airlock went flying into the crowd, bouncing and rolling to a stop at the feet of the colonists.

The people looked dumbly at the creamy white spheres on the black ground. The guards forgot about us; they, too, stared at the pearls. Selassie pulled the rags from his mouth and shouted, "See! Your trusted leaders have kept some jewels for their own private stash. So much for share and share alike in the New Order!"

Every eye was on Selassie now; every ear hung on his words. I removed my gag and took over. "That's not all, comrades! Look in the shed next to the airlock. You'll find an escape bubble the two comrades plan to use this very night. It contains the treasure you've toiled for in the mines. Your leaders plan to flee because water has begun to seep into the mine. Any day or hour now, the tunnel wall will burst, and a great flood will well up from the mine and fill the crystal dome! You'll drown in your glass fishbowl while your leaders escape with your wealth. Don't take my word for it: look in the storage shed, look in the mine."

The guards had already searched the shed while I was speaking. They came out grim-faced, holding bags of bloodstones. "Sinbad and Selassie are right about the escape bubble!" they shouted. Without another word, the guards seized the First and Second Comrades and shoved them into the middle of the angry crowd. But before the enraged colonists could do their fallen leaders any harm, a young man came running from the mine.

"It's true—there's water in the mine! It's already chest deep in the tunnel! Come quickly; we must seal the shaft before the water rises into the dome!"

The mob stampeded toward the mine, and we were left alone with the First and Second Comrades. It was now or never. I grabbed Selassie by the arm and hurried him to the shed. I expected the two comrades to follow us and fight for the escape bubble, but they did not. We carried the crystal sphere into the airlock, bolted the inner door, and pushed the pump button. We climbed into the sphere and closed the hatch as water began to rise in the chamber. As we looked back into the dome, we saw the First and Second Comrades tussling over the bags of bloodstones. So that was why they hadn't fought us for the escape vessel: even in the face of catastrophe, greed overpowered good sense.

When the chamber had filled with water, the outer door opened automatically, and we were able to maneuver the glass ball out of the dome. Buoyed up by the air within, our craft rose slowly through black waters. How wonderful it was to see the sea above us grow light and then to break through into glorious sunlight as we reached the surface! As we bobbed up and down under the blessed open sky, each of us offered up a prayer of thanks—I to Allah, and Selassie to Jesus.

"I hope the colonists were able to stop up the mine shaft and keep the dome from flooding," said Selassie. "They weren't good people, but drowning inside that great crystal dome would be a terrible way to die. So far from the sun, from other people, from God!"

"Even if they do manage to plug up the mine and keep the ocean from pouring in, they won't give credit to Allah," I replied. "They'll think they saved themselves by their own heroic efforts."

"If only they had a Bible in a language they could read, some of them would believe the truth," Selassie mused. "Faith comes by hearing the Word of God."

"But what is the Word of God," I retorted, "the Bible or the Koran?"

"Don't Muslims believe that the Bible is the Word of God, too?" asked Selassie.

"Yes, we do, though we believe that Jews and Christians corrupted it. Still, we do believe it contains much truth from Allah. It's too bad you lost your Bible in our escape. I confess I would like to hear what it has to say about the prophets."

"Oh no, Sinbad, I didn't lose my Bible." With those words, Selassie pulled his Bible out of his sash and triumphantly held it up for me to see. "The comrades left it with me—maybe they wanted to watch the octopuses tear it page from page as they were tearing me limb from limb, or maybe God kept their eyes from seeing it. Certainly, it is God's grace that I still have it. When we reach a safe place, I'll read part of it to you if you'd like."

"*If* we reach a safe place, you mean," I replied wryly. "We've escaped from the New Order, but look where we are, adrift in the middle of the ocean. There's no land in sight, not even the mad prophet's island. We can't paddle this ball, and the sun is making it quite hot. We'll probably die of sunstroke before nightfall. We must resign ourselves to the will of God. It is our *qismat*, our fate."

But being baked to death by the sun was not the lot God had determined for us. I had scarcely finished predicting our miserable end when a ship came into view on the far horizon. We couldn't shout or wave inside the glass ball and were much too far away to make ourselves known anyway. But the ball itself proclaimed our presence. Like a shining star, the crystal sphere reflected the brilliance of the midday sun in all directions. The ship saw the gleaming ball from afar and altered its course to investigate.

So it was that, within an hour, we found ourselves standing on the deck of an India-bound merchant dhow talking with our rescuers. They could scarcely believe our tale.

"A city inside a giant crystal dome undersea?" they scoffed. "The sun has addled your brains. It's true that there's an island not far from here where dwells a mad prophet, the Island of Mokat. Mariners avoid that island if possible, for the prophet and his disciples have been known to carry off poor seamen who stray from their landing party. If all you say is true, God has delivered you from two great perils. From perils and from pearls!" The sailors all laughed at their shipmate's pun.

"Truly, he did deliver us," I replied. "And we are grateful to him even though we have no pearls and no bloodstones to show for all the tribulation we've undergone. We would be very grateful if you would let us join your crew until you reach India."

"As it happens, we are two hands short," said the captain. "Two of the crew died on the outward voyage; it was their qismat. We buried them at sea. You can take their place. We'll pay you each a sequin a day. We should reach India in a month, so that would be thirty sequins each. If we like your work, you can sail with us on our return voyage to Jeddah. Jeddah is our home port."

"Why, that would be wonderful!" I exclaimed. "We were headed for Jeddah originally before we were, uh, caught in a tempest." I thought it prudent not to mention that both Selassie and I had been cast overboard by the crewmen of that ship, nor did I inform them that Selassie was a Christian. What they didn't know wouldn't hurt us.

That night Selassie and I sat on deck under a ceiling of stars and talked about God, qismat, and the Bible. Selassie began by asking about qismat:

"We Christians believe God controls all events, just as you Muslims do. But what is this qismat you've been talking about?"

"Why, it is the destiny that Allah decrees for us."

Selassie persisted in his questioning: "Do a person's good and bad deeds determine his qismat?"

"Yes and no; I mean, I'm not sure," I confessed. "We Muslims believe Allah can do whatever he pleases. He commands obedience and promises blessing for obedience, but he is not obliged to reward our obedience. We believe he is compassionate and merciful, but he can choose not to be compassionate and merciful and can even do us evil despite our good deeds if he wishes. I must admit that I can't say that a person's deeds always fix his qismat, even though I undertook this voyage in the hope of pleasing Allah by obeying all his commands."

I felt uncomfortable in admitting this to Selassie but more anxious inside as I fully realized for the first time that even perfect submission to the Koran did not guarantee Allah's favor.

"The Bible tells us about God's favor, Sinbad; it tells how and why he favors us. May I share it with you?"

"I guess so."

Selassie opened up the Bible with the strange Ethiopian letters and began to read, translating into Arabic.

> Blessed be the God and Father of our Lord Jesus Christ, who has blessed us in Christ with every spiritual blessing in the heavenly places, even as he chose us in him before the foundation of the world, that we should be holy and blameless before him. In love he predestined us for adoption through Jesus Christ, according to the purpose of his will, to the praise of his glorious grace.

As Selassie read from the Bible, my heart started beating faster. Holy and blameless in his sight! How wonderful it would be to be holy and blameless before Allah! But that was impossible: I had already committed many sins. Surely Allah has a record of all my deeds, the bad as well as the good. My hope, uncertain now, was not for blamelessness but simply that my good deeds would outweigh my bad deeds on the Day of Judgment.

But Christians sin too. How dare they think they can be holy and blameless before God? The words Selassie read moved me strangely, but I couldn't understand how they could be true nor how anyone could believe that he was holy and blameless.

Selassie saw the perplexity on my face and went on to explain the meaning of the words he had just read. His eyes shone with joy and confidence as he spoke.

"The Bible teaches that God determined the destiny of Christian believers even before he made the world. Out of love, he resolved to make us his sons through the work of his Son, Jesus Christ. We don't gain the blessings of paradise by being obedient and holy; it's our predestined end to be made holy by Christ. This isn't a matter of qismat. If I understand you rightly, qismat doesn't depend on Allah's love or holiness but only on his will, which can change—and who can call him to account for that? But the Bible says that God is unchangeable in every way, including his love."

Selassie leafed through his Bible and read the following words to me:

> Do not be deceived, my beloved brothers. Every good gift and every perfect gift is from above, coming down from the Father of lights, with whom there is no variation or shadow due to change. Of his own will he brought us forth by the word of truth.

"There you go again, talking about God's son," I said, angry and a little bewildered. "It's all very interesting, even intriguing, but you can't expect me to believe that God has a son. And I have other objections. What about those who aren't Christian believers? Did God predestine that too? We'll have to continue this discussion another day."

I was disturbed by the words Selassie had read, yet strangely thrilled. A God who loved people before they ever were, who acted to make them holy and who would never change his mind about that—if God were really like that, there would be hope for me! But how could I believe that God had a son, a son who died shamefully on the cross, when the Koran denied all of that?

Chapter 11

"You Are My Only Hope!"

With stiff monsoon breezes pushing us eastward, we arrived at the coast of India in only three weeks. We had made good time, but it was in the wrong direction. Selassie was downcast the whole way. As we stood at the rail and looked at the green hills of Malabar tumbling down to meet the sea, I noticed a single tear running down Selassie's cheek. He saw me watching and quickly wiped it away.

"Sinbad, we're going east when we want to go west. Will I ever see my home and my family again? Will I ever be able to worship God with other Christians again? I miss my family and the company of my Christian brothers and sisters so much! Not that you aren't a good friend," he added quickly, and shot an anxious look at me, "but you know what I mean. You must miss your family too."

"I have few family at present, Selassie. My wife and I were childless, and she died a year ago. My parents also are dead. I do miss my brothers and sisters. I admit that sometimes I do get lonely. Maybe that's why I'm continually drawn back to the sea. The adventure of faraway places fills me, and then I don't think about being alone."

"I love adventure as much as any boy," Selassie replied, "but it doesn't seem as wonderful at night when I lie on deck and think of my family and my country. I guess I'm especially sad now because those green hills remind me of Ethiopia.

"But when I get sad like this, I try to remember that the Lord is with me wherever I go, even to the ends of the earth. The Bible has wonderful promises for God's people, promises for every kind of fix we can get into. Maybe I'll never see my family again, but God is still with me. And I think I will see them again, somehow."

With those words, Selassie managed a brave smile that seemed real. Then our conversation ended all at once as the captain ordered all men to their stations. A watchtower on a rocky point off our bow meant that the city of Ernakulam, our destination, was at hand.

We glided past the watchtower, and the city came into view on the port bow. Houses, bazaars, piers, and temples of every color and hue ringed the harbor. Even from the mouth of the bay, we could make out carved and painted gods perched on roofs and porches. This was no whitewashed Arab city with mosques and minarets but the home of Hindus. Selassie gaped at the sight.

After we docked, the captain lined us all up and paid us off. "You're free to eat and sleep on board ship if you want. I've got to find buyers for the cargo and purchase goods for the return trip." His eyes narrowed shrewdly. "If you are inclined to do the same, there'll be room for your goods at a modest charge."

"Let's look around the city, Sinbad. I've never seen any place like this!"

"As you wish," I answered calmly. "I've been in Indian cities before, and this one is no different, but I admit that I was as excited as you the first time I set foot in such a strange place. I'll help you invest your sequins in some trade goods that will bring you profit back in Jeddah."

Selassie set off from the dock so fast that I had to run to catch up with him. We soon found ourselves in the market district. My friend delighted in the sights of the market: snake charmers, *fakirs* lying on beds of nails, humpbacked Brahmin cattle walking right through shops and eating from any vegetable cart they wanted. And the smells! At every corner, the mouth-watering odors of a half-dozen different kinds of curry mingled with the acrid smell of the charcoal burners that kept the curries bubbling. In the Street of Carpenters, the subtle fragrance of freshly carved teak, acacia, and sandalwood filled the air. Selassie seemed to forget his sadness, at least for a time. I steered him in the direction of the spice market. I intended to invest my sequins in cloves, nutmeg, and cinnamon. Spices don't take up much space and always bring a rich return in Baghdad. For all his excitement, Selassie kept an eye out for bargains.

I couldn't interest my friend in spices. "I need something smaller to carry with me, Sinbad. I'll have to walk hundreds of miles from the Horn of Africa to reach my home in Ethiopia, and a backpack of spices would be too large and too easy for others to steal. I need something I can carry in secret on my person."

"Then the only thing for you is jewels," I stated. "Come, the goldsmiths and jewelers are down this street."

We went from one goldsmith to another, inspecting their wares. Finally, Selassie selected a delicately carved gold ring. I didn't help him bargain, for he offered and counteroffered skillfully for a boy his age and obtained the ring for a fair price.

"What do you think, Sinbad? What will this fetch in Jeddah?"

A dignified, bearded young man in the robe of an official interrupted before I could congratulate Selassie on his purchase. "Sinbad? Are you Sinbad the Sailor, whose fame has spread even to our tropic shores?"

"I am," I replied with all the modesty I could muster.

"Forgive me for interrupting, but my name is Trangaram. I am a friend of Prince Vishnipim, the sovereign of this country. He is simply mad about your exploits. In his name, I should like to invite you to dine at the palace tonight. The prince would so enjoy hearing of your latest adventures. And I might add that he will send you away with a small gift, as he does all his special guests."

"We would be most honored to dine with the prince," I said.

"You may send your slave back to your ship. My master has many servants to attend to your needs."

"Selassie is not a slave; he is my friend. And he has undergone all my recent adventures with me."

Trangaram smiled. "Why then, he is welcome as a guest also. You may follow me now if it is convenient."

We certainly had no other invitations or appointments to keep, so we set off after Trangaram. Selassie and I pushed and elbowed our way through the teeming bazaar, struggling to keep up with our guide, but we had not gone a hundred feet before we lost him in the crowd. I wasn't at all concerned, for the prince's palace was in plain view all the while. Like an ornate ivory crown, it topped an emerald-green hill rising high east of the city. Its intricate windows, doors, pillars, and terraces gleamed dazzling white in the strong noonday sun. We didn't even try to find Trangaram in the crowd but made straight for the palace.

Our guide was waiting for us at the foot of an ivory staircase that swept up the hillside in graceful switchbacks. "I knew you would find your way here quickly, Sinbad," he said as he rose to his feet. "Even when you are lost in the uncharted sea, you always arrive at your desired haven in the end." I bowed, smiling, and Selassie and I followed the man up the stairs.

Slightly out of breath, we arrived at a set of double doors decorated with more carved ivory and inlaid with gold. A pair of servants in green and gold livery opened the doors, and we entered Prince Vishnipim's palace.

The prince's dwelling was even more splendid within than without. The walls were paneled with ebony, mahogany, acacia, and other rich, rare woods. Lattices of rosewood filigree between the panels allowed the sea breeze and dappled sunlight to fill the hall. Columns of veined marble, grainy porphyry, and smoky quartz supported a ceiling of aromatic cedar beams and planks. To my disgust, the carved columns bore the images of a hundred Hindu gods. What idolaters these Hindus were!

The rest of the scene was more to my liking. Thick Persian carpets covered the floor; colorful silk cushions and bolsters surrounded low brass tables where a sumptuous meal already lay prepared. With a wave of his hand, Trangaram bade us recline on the cushions. "Prince Vishnipim will join us in just a minute. Till then, why don't we enjoy some sweet tea?"

All this time, Selassie had been gazing and gaping at the walls, ceiling, and furnishings of the palace. Finally, he whispered a question: "Sinbad, I've been in the palace of Menelik, our king, but it can't compare with this! Does the Caliph in Baghdad live in such luxury?"

"That's hard to say," I replied. "The Caliph's dwelling is larger and grander, but the prince's palace is constructed of costlier materials and displays finer craftsmanship."

"And that is as it should be," said a voice behind us. We turned our heads to gaze on a handsome, beardless young man wearing a white turban and a cloth-of-gold robe. A diamond the size of an egg hung from a silver chain around his neck. "The Caliph rules a great empire and should dwell in a large house, while I am prince of but a small state, though a prosperous one." Selassie and I rose at once and bowed low.

"Make yourselves comfortable," said the prince as he reclined on the other side of the table. "You are not my subjects but free men and guests. I invited you here as those I wish to make my friends. Let us eat and drink and enjoy the evening."

With that, we began to dine. Broiled fish was the first course, ocean bass covered with a sauce made from tropical fruits unknown to me. My, it was delicious! A selection of curries followed: a mild yellow curry of lamb and chickpeas, a blistering hot red chicken curry, and a cold green vegetable curry to soothe the palate. A plate of passion fruit, mango, guava, and bananas, with coconut and tamarind dipping sauces, served as the perfect dessert.

The servants moved silently and efficiently as they supplied each new course, took away the empty dishes, and kept our cups filled with tea. Selassie and I tried not to overeat, but it was a great effort: up till that night, we had supped poorly most days and not at all on others.

When the servants had cleared away the remains of the feast and we were sipping a cup of jasmine tea, the prince turned to Selassie.

"So, young man, you find my palace more splendid than that of your own king?"

"More splendid? Yes, Your Highness, more splendid indeed. But, if you permit me to say so, not more agreeable."

"Ah, you are homesick, eh? No palace like home—do you get the joke? No place like home, no palace like home!" The prince threw his head back and laughed at his own pun, the laughter echoing in the high-ceilinged hall.

Selassie smiled weakly at the prince's joke. "It's not that, Your Highness. It's the images of your many gods carved on the pillars and painted on the ceiling that I don't find agreeable. I'm a Christian, and my country is a Christian country. We worship the one true God and abhor idols. I hope my frank words don't offend you."

"No, I'm not offended. I'm familiar with Christian beliefs, for we have Mar Thoma Christians in our own country. I get along fine with them, for we Hindus are tolerant of other faiths. We believe there are many roads to God. Yours, Sinbad's, mine—all lead to the same God. I imagine you don't find Sinbad's religion quite as bad as mine: Muslims worship only one God, like you Christians."

"Sinbad and I have talked about our differences," my friend replied. "Jesus said that he alone is the Way, the Truth, and the Life, that no one comes to God except through him. Muslims believe that Jesus was a prophet and taught the truth of God, but they don't know that he came to save us from our sins and lead us to God and eternal life. Sinbad knows that I wish for nothing more than that he should become a Christian too; I desire that even more than I long to return to my country and my family. Sinbad doesn't believe as I do yet, but I ask God every day to open his eyes and give him faith. I will pray for you too."

"Jesus claimed to be the only way to God?" asked the prince with surprise. "We Hindus believe there are many gods. Just as there are many men, some good and some evil, so there are many gods too, some good and some evil. Can Jesus be the way to all the gods?"

I said nothing during this give-and-take, but I was growing restless in my spirit. I wasn't used to hearing ideas about God that didn't agree with what I had been taught from childhood. The prince's ideas didn't bother me, for I knew there was only one God and that there could be only one way to God. But Selassie's replies disturbed and vexed me greatly. We Muslims recognized Jews and Christians as People of the Book who had received the Word of God. We believed that Jesus was a great prophet, as Selassie told the prince. But we were sure that Christians had corrupted the message of Jesus.

But what if those early Christians had *not* changed the Book? What if they really had the true teachings of the prophet Jesus? And what if Jesus was *more* than a prophet? I didn't want to think about these questions, but I couldn't shake them off.

"There is no God but Allah, and Muhammad is his prophet!" I asserted loudly, trying to drive away the doubts that had appeared, like unwanted guests, at the door of my mind.

Prince Vishnipim smiled blandly. "Perhaps we should speak of other things. This conversation could become too heated."

"As you wish," agreed Selassie. Changing the subject, my friend asked, "Your Highness, have you ever visited these Mar Thoma Christians to learn more about Jesus?"

"Only once, Selassie, after a cyclone destroyed one of their villages. I came with food and clothing for the survivors. But we found no one left alive to talk to, so I was unable to learn anything about them. Someday, when it is more convenient, I will visit these Mar Thoma Christians. After all, they, too, are my subjects."

Prince Vishnipim turned to me and opened his mouth to speak. I expected him to ask me to recount one of my many adventures, but his words surprised me.

"Sinbad, I must confess that I was overjoyed when Trangaram showed up with you for dinner. Sinbad, I desperately need your help—you are my only hope!"

Chapter 12
Zaza Fruit

"There must be some mistake, Your Highness!" I replied with astonishment. "I am a simple merchant who's always getting into one scrape after another. Why Allah has permitted me to escape with my life time and time again, I have no idea. I'm the one always in need of help; I don't see how I could help you or anyone else."

Tears started from the prince's eyes as he replied in a quavering voice, "When you hear my story, you will see why I hope you can help me."

"Please tell us your story, Prince."

"I'll try to tell it without breaking down, but my bitterness of soul is so great that I don't know if I can. Still, here it is:

"A year ago, while on a state visit to the city of Allepey, I fell in love with a beautiful princess, the niece of the king of Allepey. The princess fell in love with me as well. Now, you need to know that my beloved's parents were dead, and she lived with her uncle the king. It was both natural and proper for me to ask the king for his niece's hand in marriage. Allepey is smaller than Ernakulam and not as prosperous.

I was richer than my wife's uncle, so I thought he would be happy to bless our match. But I was only a prince, not a king. The old man didn't think I was good enough for his niece.

"We were so in love that we fled to Ernakulam in secret and were married anyway, against the king's wishes. When he discovered what we had done, he was furious. He sent word to us that he never wished to see her or me again.

"It was wrong for us to disobey the king, for he was my wife's uncle and guardian. She was his ward and should have obeyed him; I should have submitted to his decision. We both knew that before we married. But now our disobedience has brought punishment upon us! It is our *karma*."

"What is karma?" I asked.

"It is one's destiny. Our deeds determine our karma. The good we do is rewarded; the bad we do is punished. If a man does good in this life, he may be reborn into a higher caste; if a woman does good, she may be reborn a man. And if a man does evil, he may be reborn as a lower-caste man, a woman, or even an animal. But sometimes bad deeds bring bad karma in the same life, and that is what has happened to my poor wife and me."

I said nothing but thought plenty. What a repulsive doctrine! These Hindus believe we pass through many lives and never come to final judgment. Rewards and punishments are just stages to . . . well, maybe to nothing. Those rebirths could go on forever! I wondered what a Christian thought of all this.

"Selassie," I asked, "Do Christians believe in karma?

"No," he replied. "First of all, we believe we have only one life to live under the sun. Second, it's true that the way we live may bring blessing or woe in this life, but sometimes it doesn't. Some men and women live godly lives and suffer; some live evil lives and prosper. The sufferings of this life are of God, but he doesn't send them on us so that we can atone for our sins through suffering. Jesus Christ suffered all the punishment his people deserve for their sins."

"But Christians suffer too, like the rest of men," interrupted the prince. "What about those Mar Thoma Christians whose village was smashed flat by the cyclone? The stench of the dead bodies buried beneath their shattered homes lasted for weeks. Men, women, and children, all killed. They must have sinned to have suffered such bad karma."

Selassie replied, "When Christians suffer in this life, even because of their own foolishness or sin, their suffering is not punishment. It is often correction meant to make us more obedient disciples of Jesus Christ. Even suffering that leads to death comes from a loving God. We trust him even when we don't understand his ways.

"As for the suffering of those who are not Christians, it's a merciful warning, a taste of the punishment they will receive on the great Judgment Day if they don't turn to Christ in repentance and faith."

"I would gladly heed any warning your God has for me, Selassie, if only he would take away my great punishment!" cried out the prince.

"I'm sorry we interrupted you, Your Highness," I quickly replied. "We haven't given you a chance to tell us what terrible thing happened to you. Please continue with your story."

"The great blow fell only a week after we married. I was showing my beloved the palace grounds, and we went into the rose garden. She let out a cry of delight when she caught sight of a bush in the middle of the garden bearing dozens of perfect golden roses. Those roses weren't just golden in color; their petals flamed with the metallic luster of pure gold. My bride asked me what kind of roses they were. I confessed that I didn't know: I'd never noticed the bush before, remarkable though it was. My beloved picked a perfect rosebud to smell its sweet perfume, but in doing so, she pricked her finger. Instantly she fell down in a faint. My bodyguards, a few paces behind as always, rushed to pick her up. I ordered them to carry her into the palace and lay her on her bed. Surely she merely fainted at the sight of blood, I thought; she will soon awaken from her swoon.

"That was nearly a year ago. My poor, sweet wife hasn't opened her eyes since that terrible day. I call her name, imploring her to wake, but she doesn't answer! My beloved is as lost to me as if she had died, yet she lies in my palace as lovely as ever! The images that assault her while she slumbers and the anguish of my heart are certainly our karma."

At this, the prince broke down completely and sobbed. After a time, pulling himself together, he was able to go on.

"There is a little more to tell. Naturally, I wondered if the gardener had put some poison on the rose to kill insects, some poison that might have been on the thorn. He told me that the fatal rosebush had arrived on our wedding day. It was a gift, he explained, sent by the king of Allepey, my wife's uncle. The gardener showed me a letter in the king's own hand stating that the rose was a favorite of his niece and should be planted in the palace garden as a wedding surprise for her. I knew then that the wicked old man had revenged himself on us for defying his wishes. I wrote him again and again, pleading with him to tell me what potion or venom he had painted on the thorn and begging him to send an antidote. He has never replied.

"So when I heard you were coming to dinner, Sinbad, I was overjoyed. You have been to so many strange lands and seen so many wonderful things. Do you know of a golden rose with the power to lay people in an endless sleep? Do you know a cure?"

I scratched my head and tried to think. I brought before my mind all the things that had happened to me on my seven voyages, all the marvelous things I'd seen.

"I'm so sorry, Highness, but I've never encountered such a thing in all my travels. Selassie, have you such roses in Ethiopia?"

"No, Sinbad, not to my knowledge. Of course, I've never paid much attention to roses. But I'd like to see this rosebush. Maybe I'll recognize it after all."

The prince, weeping softly again, rose to his feet and, with a wave of his hand, indicated that we should follow him; he was too broken up to speak. We left the banqueting room, crossed a terrace, and descended a short set of marble steps into a sunken garden.

The sun was just setting over the far end of the garden. Its fiery beams reflected off a bush in the midst of the garden with such brilliance that we had to cover our eyes. That had to be the beautiful, deadly rosebush sent by the wicked king. In a very few minutes, the tropical sun had plunged into the bay, and we could examine the bush in the cool light of the rising moon. I rolled a golden rosebud around in my fingers, taking special care not to prick myself with a thorn. Selassie squatted down and examined the stem and branches; then, he plucked a leaf and peered at it intently, carefully turning it over to examine both front and back.

My friend rose to his feet. "Sinbad," he said, "This isn't a living rosebush. It's the product of skilled craftsmen, a woodcarver and a goldsmith, at least."

"And an apothecary who can mix potions to be painted on thorns," I added.

I turned to the prince. "Your Highness, although you should have respected the king's wishes, what he did was desperately cruel and wicked. Selassie and I will seek out the makers of this piece and find out, by bribery or threat if necessary, what kind of elixir was painted on the thorn and what the antidote may be. We will do what we can for you and your bride."

We carefully removed several thorns from the rosebush. Then we took leave of the prince, who was still too overcome with woe to speak. We returned to the ship for the night.

The next morning we went into the city to find the Bazaar of Apothecaries, those skilled in preparing elixirs, potions, and medicines. The captain, who knew Ernakulam well, told us to seek out a certain graybeard named Vijay.

"You say you're interested in elixirs? Go to old Vijay. The inhabitants of the city know him well, and not a few fear him. The superstitious are convinced that he's a sorcerer. You and I know better. Old Vijay prepares herbal extracts with all sorts of powers. What that old man doesn't know about the virtues of leaves and roots isn't worth knowing."

We found Vijay the apothecary without difficulty and explained what we were looking for. "These thorns are coated with a sleeping potion of some sort. We want to know what it is and purchase the antidote."

The old man silently took a single thorn, placed it in a cup of water, and set it on a brazier of glowing charcoal. Soon the water began to boil. Vijay grasped the cup with tongs and set it on the side of the brazier to simmer. After a few minutes, the apothecary removed the cup from the flame. I looked in the cup and saw a golden broth. Vijay sniffed the steam rising from the broth and nodded his head. Then he unlocked a wooden cabinet, which proved to contain a hundred or more bottles, each filled with a colored powder or liquid. None of the bottles had a label, but the old man knew them all by sight. Without hesitation, he picked a bottle of red powder from the collection, uncorked it, and sprinkled just a pinch in the cup of hot water. The water instantly turned black.

The apothecary smiled and turned to us. "I thought as much when I smelled the vapors, but the red-powder test removes all doubt. The potion on the thorns was made from the juice of the golden zaza fruit. The antidote is a drink made from the juice of the purple zaza fruit. That will be fifty rupees, please."

"We would like to buy a portion of the antidote, please."

The old man's face grew dark. "I cannot help you with that. I have none; no apothecary in Ernakulam has any. The zaza tree, with its golden and purple fruit, grows only in the jungles of Allepey, and the king of Allepey forbids its export. As if that were not enough, the great black apes of Allepey love zaza fruit. It doesn't affect them the way it affects human beings; to the apes, it's more like candy. Each ape has his own tree, which he guards jealously day and night to keep other creatures away. Those apes can tear you limb from limb. Few are the men daring enough to try to gather zaza fruit. I've obtained small quantities of both fruits only a few times in my long life. I have none now. Who obtained the golden fruit and made the potion painted on that thorn?"

We told old Vijay we didn't know, paid him his fifty rupees, and left. We now knew what we had to do to cure the prince's bride: make our way to Allepey, go into the jungle and find a zaza tree, pick some purple fruit, return to Ernakulam, and prepare an elixir to awaken the princess. Of course, we had to avoid detection by the king's soldiers and the black apes that keep ceaseless watch over their trees. It wouldn't be easy. In fact, the more I contemplated the task ahead, the more impossible it appeared.

We set out for Allepey that very afternoon. I proposed to pass myself off as a merchant seeking tiger skins; that would provide cover for going into the jungle. Selassie would play the part of my slave. The prince furnished us with three horses and a bag of money. The third horse was supposedly to carry the tiger skins we would buy in the villages.

As soon as we were underway, Selassie began to talk. "I'm puzzled, Sinbad. I don't understand how the *karma* of the Hindus is different from the *qismat* you Muslims talk about. Are they the same thing?"

I was surprised and shocked at Selassie's remark. "They aren't at all alike, Selassie; why would you think that?"

"Well, the prince thinks his karma must come to pass as a result of his wrongdoing; there's nothing he can do to avoid or change it. And you believe the same about your qismat: nothing can be done to alter it either, since God decreed it. If that's true, we have no business trying to help the prince and princess."

"Selassie, we don't know what the prince and princess's qismat is. True, if Allah has decided that she is to remain asleep till Judgment Day, we can do nothing to change it—but we don't know that." I stopped and stared directly into Selassie's eyes. "Are you trying to back out of this affair?"

"Not at all!" my friend shot back. "I want to press on, and I have good hope for success. You see, I don't believe in karma or qismat. As I told you, Christians don't believe that we must pay for our sins by suffering in this life, as the Hindus do. It's true, we believe that God decreed all that must take place before the world began, but that's not the same as qismat. God invites his children to pray that he will make events turn out this way or that. He encourages us to seek good and right things from him, the way a child seeks good things from his father. God is our Father. He has promised in his Word, the Bible, to answer the prayers his children offer up in Jesus's name, so long as our prayers agree with his will made known in the Bible.

"So I think it's right to ask God to give us success in our endeavor because it is a good thing we are trying to do. Fathers want to help their children succeed in good undertakings. Sinbad, do Muslims ever think of God as their father and pray to him as children coming to a loving father?"

"No, Allah is far too high to be approached with such familiarity," I replied. The conversation drifted to other things, but I couldn't get Selassie's question out of my mind. I was always trying so hard, trying to please a distant God but never knowing if he was satisfied with my efforts. I felt a sudden longing for God to be close to me and to love me like a father. Islam offered no hope of that, and for the first time, I knew Selassie, the Christian, had something I wanted.

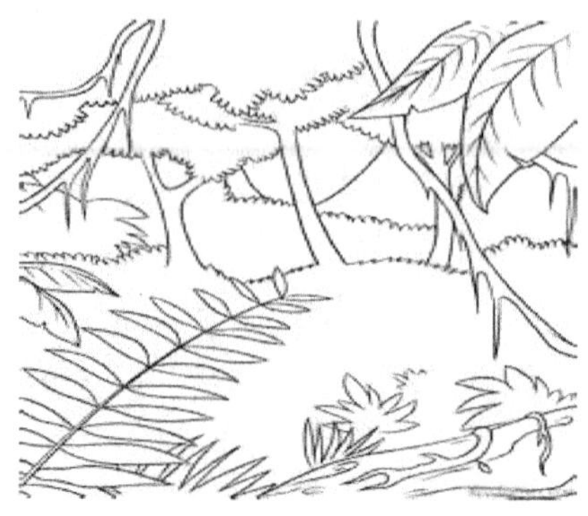

Chapter 13
A Night in the Jungle

It was a three-day journey to the kingdom of Allepey. At the border, we stopped at a little customs house beside the road and waited in line with other travelers for the king's men to question us. Finally, our turn came.

"Why do you wish to enter Allepey?" asked a portly official, clearly bored with his job.

"I am a buyer and seller of animal skins, especially tiger skins," I replied with a smile. "I intend to make the rounds of the jungle villages and purchase high-quality tiger skins to sell back in Baghdad—provided, of course, that I can obtain them at a good price."

"And who is the lad?"

"My slave. Believe me, I have no intention of selling him here. I need him to pack skins, cook, and take care of the horses."

"Very well, you may pass. We're not worried about you selling your slave; slavery is not permitted in Allepey. You do realize that when you leave our country, you will have to pay taxes on any skins you have bought."

"I'd be surprised if I didn't have to pay taxes to pass through customs," I replied with a grin. I knew that royal officials like this plump specimen made a lot of money overcharging travelers, but that didn't concern me then. The prince would pay back all our expenses and more if only we could find the fruit that would awaken his beloved wife. The customs officer waved us on. We gave our reins a flick, and our horses began to trot down the road.

In a few hours, we came to a fork in the way. The broad, main road continued south toward the city of Allepey, while a narrower dirt track branched off to the left in the direction of the hills and the jungle. We turned our horses to the left.

"Sinbad, what do we do once we reach the jungle?" Selassie asked.

I hadn't given much thought to that. "I suppose we'll stop at the first village and ask about zaza trees," I answered. "The king has forbidden the sale of zaza fruit, but a few gold sequins will bring us the information we seek if the villagers have it."

We left the flat, cultivated coast and entered the jungle as the western sun was beginning to cast long shadows. I hoped we would find a village before it got dark. I had no desire to spend the night in the jungle, alive as it was, with strange noises and hundreds of shining eyes.

But though we spurred our horses on at a good clip, night overtook us in the forest. We did manage to find a clearing beside the road before it grew too dark to go further. We bedded down there after cooking a small meal and brewing a pot of tea. The stench of rotting leaves and horse sweat overwhelmed the delicate fragrance of the tea, but we tried to ignore the smell as we sipped our evening drink.

"I suppose you have slept in the jungle before, Selassie," I said as we watched the moon rise above the shadowy jungle trees.

"A few times, Sinbad, though I am more used to sleeping in an open field under the stars when I am on a journey in my country.

Most of Ethiopia is grassy highlands. Still, I have spent nights in the jungle, as few as possible. I don't like it very much."

"I don't either. But our fire will keep the beasts away. Animals fear fire."

"Except snakes, Sinbad. And look to your right!"

I turned my head and gasped as I saw a long, yellow cobra slither out of the shadows toward the fire. I jumped up and struck it with a staff several times till I was sure I had crushed its head.

"That's enough for me!" I said. "Let's mount up and ride in the dark. There's enough moonlight to make our way forward."

"And if we should meet a tiger or panther hunting for its meal?"

"They can find us as easily here as on the road," I said, "and at least the snakes won't bother us while we're riding."

"True enough," my friend agreed, and with that, we packed up our goods (after making sure no snake had crawled into them to find a cozy bed) and saddled the horses. Soon we were riding slowly down the jungle path by the light of the moon. The thick, shiny leaves of the jungle foliage gleamed like soft silver on both sides of the path. We rode in silence, drinking in the quiet beauty of the night. Even the monkeys had ceased their chattering.

The moon was almost overhead, and we had just ridden around a curve when I heard a soft *clip-clop* behind us. Selassie and I looked at each other at the same time. His eyes widened in alarm, an alarm I felt too. Whoever was out on such a night was not likely to be up to any good. I put a finger on my lips and turned my horse aside into the trees; Selassie followed. I forced my unwilling horse into the black forest till I knew we could not be seen from the path.

Not a moment too soon! A dozen men on mules trotted into view. Flashes of moonlight from the swords and daggers they bore stabbed into the forest as if seeking to skewer us. We could not be seen, of course, but we felt exposed, like geckos on a wall. The robbers—for that is what they clearly were—stopped right where we had turned aside. Had they seen us leave the trail? The leader held up a hand for silence and cocked his head as though listening for the fearful pounding of our hearts.

After a few seconds—they seemed like hours—one of the men spoke. "I don't hear nothing, Chief. Are you sure there was horses ahead of us?"

"You question me? Of course I heard horses. All of you, get down and look for prints."

The robber band had ridden right over our tracks, and at first, I thought that they might not discover us. But one of the robbers stood up with a cry of triumph. "Look, here's a tuft of horsehair on this branch. I'll bet they went into the trees right here."

"Then they must have heard us," replied the one they called Chief. "Nobody would go into the jungle here in the dark if he wasn't afraid for his life."

"Not if they knowed where they was, they wouldn't," cackled the finder of the horsehair.

"We'll go in after them, boys, and run these foxes to ground," said the chief. "There's enough of us that the hairy ones won't bother us. Light a torch, every man, and draw your sword. Whether or not they have anything worth stealing, we can't have people running 'round who know we're here."

Selassie and I were in a tight spot. We couldn't outrun or outfight a dozen men. Maybe we could hide. I gestured silently to Selassie to dismount. "We'll send the horses off one way while we go in the other direction," I whispered. "Those thugs will follow the horses. By the time they catch them and realize we went another way, we'll have made our escape."

We swatted the horses across the rump, and they bolted away, crashing noisily through the trees. Turning away from them, we plunged deeper into the inky woods, not knowing what lay ahead. My friend and I stumbled through the trees, twisting this way and that as we fought off clinging vines and grasping branches that seemed bent on seizing and holding us for the robbers. Just enough moonlight filtered down to the jungle floor to reveal fallen logs that might trip us or catch us up.

We ran till we came to a stream. It was too wide to jump, and the jungle was too dark to chance wading. Who knew how deep it might be or if a crocodile might be floating like a log, patiently waiting for a deer so heedless as to attempt a midnight drink? We had no choice but to turn and follow the bank upstream. Perhaps the water would narrow and we would be able to leap over the water.

Ahead of us, lights began to bob up and down, approaching with an unhurried pace. The robbers had circled around and were closing in from the other side! We turned to flee back downstream, only to see more lights coming from that direction. Wheeling to flee away from the water, we saw more of the accursed torches. The cutthroats had found and surrounded us. They were closing in, moving slowly and deliberately, beating the bushes to flush us out of any holes where we might have taken refuge. They would be on top of us in a few minutes.

"I will say of the Lord, 'He is my refuge and my fortress, my God, in whom I trust.' You will not fear the terror of night." Selassie, eyes closed, was speaking softly.

"What are you talking about?" I whispered fiercely. "Do you want them to find us even more quickly?"

"I'm reciting words of comfort from the Bible, Sinbad. I admit I do fear the terror that stalks us tonight, but when I speak God's Word to myself, I don't feel nearly so afraid. God uses his Word to create faith."

"Do you think your God will reach down from heaven and snatch you away from the doom closing in on us?" I asked sarcastically. Then a large hand grasped my collar and lifted me straight up into the air.

Chapter 14
The Hairy Ones

I shut my eyes in fear and dared not open them.

"O great God, I am sorry for my blasphemy!" I babbled. "I had no idea you would really reach down from heaven and snatch me up. Selassie is my good friend; be merciful to me for his sake." I continued to blubber, saying I knew not what, till the hand that gripped me lifted me up and set me on a pair of hairy shoulders.

I opened my eyes and saw that it was not God who bore me away from the astonished robbers but a great, black ape! So these were the hairy ones the robber spoke of! The creature was leaping and swinging through the jungle canopy hand over hand. I clutched its long, coarse hair tightly, afraid that I would slip and fall. Fearfully looking around, I saw another ape behind me bearing Selassie.

I looked down to see how high we were. Beneath us, I saw only inky blackness, but I could hear roars and growls down there, the nighttime sounds of hungry jungle beasts seeking their prey. We were scarcely high enough above them to suit me, yet far too high for comfort. I closed my eyes again and continued to hold on for dear life. I couldn't see the ape's face, but its coarse, matted hair and musty body odor, more overpowering than the smell of wet dog, told me I was not being carried away from danger by an angel!

The ape hurried on, looping left and right as he swung from tree to tree but always pressing forward. It seemed we traveled for hours before we finally stopped, landing on some solid surface with such a crash that I tumbled off the ape's back. I opened my eyes once more and found myself sitting on a deck of sticks perched on the crown of a low tree. The ape, a dark hairy hulk silhouetted against the silver moonlight, sat across from me on the other end of the deck. I suppose he was looking back at me. Other shadowy trees loomed nearby. Each one was topped by a platform, the watchtower of another ape.

We must have sat facing each other in the dark for several hours before dawn came on with a rush, as it does in the tropics. In less than ten minutes, light flooded the sky, and I could see clearly. Straight rows of trees stretched for half a league in every direction. I was not in the jungle anymore but in some kind of plantation. At first, I thought the trees were all the same, for they all had the same form, the same saw-toothed olive leaves, the same pearly gray bark. But when I looked more closely, I saw that the trees were actually of two kinds. One kind bore small, smooth, yellow fruit; the other bore large, wrinkled, purple fruit. I had found it! Zaza fruit! And what good *qismat* was mine: the tree I was in sported the purple variety, the very kind we needed!

We. That little word reminded me that Selassie wasn't with me. Surely the ape that grabbed him had also hurried to the plantation; Selassie must be here too, somewhere. I stood up to look around, but the beast immediately jerked me to my knees with his shaggy paw. He pulled me across the rough wooden platform till our faces were only inches apart, baring his teeth and snarling through thick, curled lips in a manner that left no doubt as to his displeasure. The ape didn't have the use of words, but it was clear I'd better not stand up again.

I grew depressed as I considered our plight. Old Vijay had told us that the apes guard their zaza trees jealously. How could I find Selassie in that large plantation? How could we possibly escape with the purple zaza fruit? How could we possibly escape with our lives?

In the end, finding Selassie proved to be no problem at all. Even as I was despairing of my state, the crude deck of sticks began to tremble. Something was climbing up the tree! Before I had time to ponder what it might be, another ape, bigger and hairier than the one watching me, bounded onto the platform and plopped down next to my guardian. My heart skipped a beat when I saw him, for he had Selassie pinned beneath his arm! The ape released Selassie and began to chatter at his companion.

When Selassie caught sight of me, he scurried over to my side of the platform and sat down beside me. Saying not a word, we watched as the apes jabbered away at each other. They didn't talk like people do, alternately talking and listening. Instead, each chimp kept up a ceaseless stream of noise. They seemed unconcerned about us so long as we didn't try to get up on our feet. When I thought they weren't looking, I tried again to stand up, but my captor pulled me back down, not at all gently.

After a few minutes, Selassie whispered, "Sinbad, I don't think those apes understand each other any better than we understand them."

"I think you're right. In some foggy way, they know they need to do something with us, but they have no language and can't share their thoughts—if they have thoughts," I added. "To think that some philosophers believe we're nothing but highly developed apes!"

"Not Christian philosophers," replied Selassie. "The Bible teaches that we are made in the image of God."

"Even those robbers?" I asked scornfully. "Muslims don't believe in making images of Allah, and we certainly don't believe human beings were created in his image."

"Yes, Sinbad, even those robbers bear God's image. But the Bible teaches that Adam and Eve, the first man and woman, sinned by disobeying God. When they sinned, they fell from their first state. Their fall affected all their descendants. All of us are guilty before God and also corrupt in nature. The image of God is still there, but it has been defaced like a vandalized statue."

I didn't reply. We Muslims believed that humans begin life good but weak. We can become corrupt, but we can also become better. Well, that's what I was raised to think, though I'd already begun to doubt whether I could become good enough to please Allah.

I didn't have time right then to muse on these things. Our tree began to quiver and shake again as one ape after another climbed up to join our guards. All the hairy ones were chattering and gibbering without letup. We sensed they were agitated by our presence but didn't know what to do with us. The pandemonium rose to such a roar that I didn't think I could stand another minute of it. Then, all at once, sudden silence. Had the beasts decided how to dispose of us? Selassie and I looked at each other anxiously.

In the next few seconds, we found that we were entirely wrong. The apes had not fallen silent because they had come to a decision regarding us. They gestured to each other and pointed down one of the grassy aisles between the trees. At least forty men were slowly riding our way. They went hunched over, eyes scouring the ground. They never looked up to the dark treetops. Were those cutthroats looking for us? Were they lost?

Selassie and I would never know because as soon as the robbers passed under the tree, the apes leaped down on them. They dragged the men off their mules and started rolling around with them on the ground, trying to wrestle the robbers into submission. The robbers were tough men and fought back with the extraordinary strength born of desperation. Man and ape bit and gouged and kicked each other; bloody handfuls of hair flew everywhere; howls and grunts and curses filled the air. The mules neighed in panic and galloped away as fast as mules could go.

Every ape had joined the melee; not even one remained on the platform to guard us.

"Now's our chance, Selassie! Stuff some purple zaza fruit into your sash, and let's get out of here!" My friend needed no encouragement; he grabbed a handful of fruit and jumped down onto the heap of rolling, twisting bodies before I'd finished speaking. I shimmied down the trunk, and we both took to our heels. The apes and the robbers, locked in a life-and-death struggle, didn't notice us.

We had no idea where we were, but God was good to us. At the edge of the plantation, we came on a pair of mules that stood panting, unwilling to plunge into the jungle. We mounted the beasts and dug our heels into their fat bellies; they let out a startled *hee-haw* and lurched into the trees. Less than a hundred yards into the forest, a small creek cut across our way. We saw a footpath on the far bank, so we forded the sluggish, green waters and turned our mules downstream. Before the tropical sun had reached its zenith, we emerged from the trees and found that we had arrived at the road from the coast, the road we had taken into the jungle only a day before. How much had happened in that short space of night and morning!

Many travelers were on the road that day, and we felt safe. Even if the robbers escaped from the apes and followed our tracks, they wouldn't allow themselves to be seen on the road in daylight. As for the apes, they never ventured far from the trees. We had dodged disaster yet again.

As we trotted down the road to the coast, I reopened the discussion we had on the platform.

"I must insist, Selassie: the Koran teaches that Allah created man out of earth and gave him life, but Allah did not create man in his image."

"Then how are we different from apes?"

"Man is more intelligent and nobler," I confidently replied.

"Would you say that of all men? How about the robbers? I preferred the company of the apes to the tender mercies of those cutthroats."

"I've got you now, Selassie. You wouldn't say apes were created in God's image, but you prefer them to the robbers. How, then, can robbers be created in his image?"

Selassie looked at me sharply. "Sinbad, do you realize that you are talking past me, just like those two apes jabbered at each other? They didn't listen to each other; they just blurted out their own feelings. Please don't take offense at what I say, but that's how it seems to me."

I was taken aback. My friend was right. I was just asserting what I had been taught and believed without really listening to him. Maybe that was because when I did listen, I was disturbed by doubts. Well, if Islam was true, I ought not to be unwilling to weigh my friend's words. But what if Islam had no answers to Selassie's challenges? I resolved to face his arguments head-on.

All these thoughts went through my head in a few seconds. "You're right, Selassie," I replied. "I haven't listened to you with an open mind. I'm sorry; I'll do that in the future. But we don't have time to talk right now. Look, we're already almost to the border, where the king's guards will search us from head to toe. They're always on the lookout for zaza fruit; that's the one thing the king won't let out of the country. We've got to find some way to smuggle our hard-earned prize past the guards."

I felt in my sash for the zaza fruit I had stashed there, but to my dismay, I found that it was gone. It must have fallen out somewhere.

"Selassie, I've lost the zaza fruit I stuffed in my sash. I hope you have enough."

Selassie loosened his sash, and his face fell. He held up a hand of wet, purple pulp. "Sinbad! All my zaza fruit has been smashed to pieces! I suppose it happened when I jumped and landed on that squirming mass of fighting apes and robbers. What can we do with this mashed fruit? It will rot before we get back to Ernakulam."

We were in a bad way. It was impossible to return to the jungle and get more zaza fruit: either the apes or the robbers would do us in, and both would be on the watch for us. God had delivered us, but we had failed in our quest. How could we face Prince Vishnipim?

Chapter 15
The Princess Awakens

We stood by the side of the road and debated what we should do next. Selassie wanted to return to the jungle and try again, but I wouldn't hear of it.

"Let's go back to old Vijay. Maybe there is some other way to wake the princess from her slumber."

"I don't see how that could help at all," Selassie replied. "Vijay already told us that the only antidote was purple zaza fruit."

We might have stood there at a loss for hours, but *qismat* (as I thought then) stepped in.

"Hey, you!" came a voice behind us. We turned around to see a patrol of soldiers marching toward us—well, actually, they were slouching their way up the road, shoulders hunched, not looking very military at all. We waited silently till they shuffled up to us and their lieutenant spoke to me.

"You look like foreigners. Where is your home?"

"Our home is Baghdad, in the realm of the great Caliph. I am a merchant seeking to buy tiger skins. This lad is my servant."

"You don't have any tiger skins with you."

"Our mission was unsuccessful. The villagers in the jungle wanted more than I was willing to pay. We are headed to Ernakulam, where we hope prices will be lower."

"Well, that's fine. We'll escort you to the border. But first, we must search you. Our king has had word that two foreigners, a man and a boy answering to your description, have entered the kingdom in search of . . . of a product that we absolutely refuse to allow out of the country."

"What would that be?" I asked innocently.

"Never you mind about that. We intend to search you. If we find that, er, product, we'll know you are the foreigners we seek, and then woe to you! If we don't find it, we will know that you are not seeking za—I mean, the product, and we will let you go."

How glad I was then that we had no zaza fruit. Selassie had thrown his mashed fruit into a ditch a half-mile back. The men made us dismount and searched our saddle bags. They contained some food and some silver cups and plates that the robbers had been carrying. I suppose the silver was stolen. The soldiers raised their eyebrows at the silver but said nothing; silver was not what they were looking for. Then they made us disrobe, right down to our underclothes. The officer squinted at Selassie's Bible.

"What is this book, lad?"

"It is the Word of God, sir; it is the Bible."

"Never heard of it," said the man. Then he looked carefully at the purple-stained sash where Selassie had carried the Bible and the zaza fruit. The color of the stain interested him.

"How did your sash get colored purple, lad?"

I jumped in before Selassie could answer, for I knew he could never lie convincingly. "My servant was carrying some purple grapes for a snack on the road, but he tripped over a stone and fell. The grapes were smashed, so we threw them away several miles back."

The officer narrowed his eyes and grimaced. I held my breath, hoping he would buy my story. Finally, he shook his head and said, "It's too hot to stand out here and quiz you any longer. You don't have the product we're looking for, so we'll walk you to the frontier and make sure you leave the country."

The soldiers were hot and tired and not very zealous to find the strangers. We walked along silently in front of the patrol for about a mile until we reached the customs house at the border.

"We've already searched these two," the officer said to the customs guards. "They have some silver items in their saddle bags, but they're not the foreigners we've been told to apprehend." The guards, who looked as bored with their job as the soldiers, brightened up when they heard about the silver.

"You'll have to pay 20 percent of that silver as an exit fee, my friend," said the portly guard as he flashed a greasy smile and started removing the silver from the saddlebags. I didn't complain in the slightest, though I knew that the standard exit fee was only 10 percent. The guards and the soldiers would split the extra 10 percent. After we were cleared for exit, we crossed into Ernakulam. Looking over my shoulder, I saw that the soldiers had flopped down in the shade of the building as the officer and the guards argued over who would get which silver pieces. Let them have it, I thought; we're safe now.

Ernakulam had its own customs guards, but when we left the country, we had given them a letter from the prince explaining our mission, and they recognized us and let us pass without questioning. On the three-day journey back to the prince, we said very little to each other. Melancholy settled over us like a fog. We had failed the prince. What could we do?

When we reached the city gate, I again proposed that we should visit Vijay, the apothecary, before reporting to the prince.

"What have we got to lose?" I asked.

Selassie agreed with me, but discouragement was in his voice. "Very well, Sinbad, let's see Vijay first. As you say, we have nothing to lose."

"Vijay!" I called as we entered his shop. When he heard my voice, old Vijay jumped to his feet and hobbled to greet us as quickly as he could.

"Do you have the purple zaza fruit?" he rasped.

"No, Vijay, we failed." I told him the whole story of our unhappy journey into Allepey and back again. "We return with some silver and a couple of mules. Our only loss was Selassie's sash. He will have to buy a new one, since the old one is stained with purple zaza juice. But that's not important. The greatest loss is that we failed the prince."

Vijay's face lit up with a big grin. "No, you did not fail! Give me that sash!" Puzzled, Selassie untied the sash and handed it to the apothecary. Vijay set a pot of water on the charcoal brazier. When the water began boiling, he stuffed the sash down into the pot.

"Don't you understand?" he asked us. "We can boil enough juice out of the sash to prepare an elixir to wake the princess!" The old man stirred the sash around in the simmering water, and as he stirred it, the water began to turn color—first a light violet, then darker and darker purple until the potion was almost indigo. After ten minutes, he removed the pot from the brazier and let it cool. When the pot was cool enough to pick up with bare hands, he filled a small earthenware flask with the liquid and stoppered it with a wax plug.

"Take this to the palace and remove the stopper under the princess's nose. The aroma alone will wake her enough to be able to drink. Make her drink of it until she is fully awake. I am keeping the remainder of this potion as my pay. I never thought I would ever again have a supply of purple zaza elixir—how blessed we all are!"

"Truly," replied Selassie with conviction, "God has blessed us all." With that, I could heartily agree, but I wondered why God had blessed us. I didn't really think it was because I was a faithful Muslim, for by then, I knew that my good works were not enough to please God. But Selassie had said that his God blessed him without his deserving it. And the prince, who had idols in his palace, certainly didn't deserve blessing. I determined to learn why Selassie believed God blesses the undeserving. But first, we had to go to the palace and wake the princess.

We announced ourselves at the palace gate and waited. In just a few minutes, Trangaram appeared and showed us inside.

"Did you succeed? Did you find the purple zaza fruit?" he asked eagerly as he led us to the chamber where we had feasted with the prince only a week earlier.

"No," I said. "But we must report to the prince." Selassie's eyes turned as big as hen's eggs when I told Trangaram that we had not achieved our quest.

"But Sinbad!" my friend began to exclaim; I quickly clapped a hand over his mouth and said, "No, Selassie, you are not to blame. I must shoulder the failure myself."

"Trangaram," I said, turning to the prince's friend, "I'm sure you understand that we need to talk to the prince alone. He can tell you the details of our failure if he wishes, but I am too ashamed to let anyone but him hear our story."

"Of course," Trangaram replied. "I will tell the prince you are here and then retire to my own home."

When the man left us, I explained my strange conduct to Selassie.

"Selassie, do you remember how the lieutenant said that the king of Allepey had heard that two strangers, a man like me and a boy like you, were seeking zaza fruit? How could that news have reached the king? Only through an informant right here in the prince's palace! The only one who knew of our journey beside the prince himself was Trangaram. I believe he is a traitor in the pay of the king of Allepey! He it was, I am sure, who put the poisoned golden rosebush in the garden where the princess would find it and, as he knew well, prick her finger. If Trangaram knew we had succeeded, he would find some way to steal the elixir or perhaps do away with the princess or even the prince! Not only must we wake the princess, but we must warn the prince before Trangaram becomes suspicious."

At that moment, the prince entered the room. Trembling, he asked me, "Sinbad, do you have the purple zaza fruit?"

"No," I said loudly, but I nodded my head yes. "We failed, for we were unable to bring zaza fruit from Allepey," I said in a voice loud enough that anyone lurking outside the chamber door could hear me. But as I spoke, I pointed silently to the flask of elixir, which I pulled out of my robe. Selassie was not idle; he wrote a short explanation on the writing tablet the prince kept by his side. The prince read the message, then nodded.

I raised my voice and continued: "I should like to see the sleeping princess before I depart in sadness for my native land."

"Yes, I will take you to her," the prince said loudly and led us through a side door into an inner corridor. When we reached the end of the corridor, the prince unlocked an ornately carved door and led us into the room where the princess lay sleeping. She was beautiful indeed! I could see why the prince had risked the king of Allepey's wrath by eloping with her.

I did just what Vijay said. Removing the wax stopper, I held the flask under the princess's nose. She sighed and struggled to sit up. "Drink this, Your Highness," I said as I held the flask to her lips. Eyes still closed, the princess took a sip of the elixir. She opened her eyes and smiled as she saw her husband's joyful yet anxious face; then she took another drink. That was all it took. The young woman stood up, yawned and stretched, then tenderly kissed her husband.

"I slept so well last night, my love," she said to him. "I feel so rested. But I feel so lazy, too. I imagine you have been up for hours—the sun is already at noon!"

"I'll tell you all about it in a little while," the prince answered. The man really had no choice; he was too choked up to speak.

"My dear, who is this man with us? Who is the boy?"

"That, too, must wait for a little while," the prince said. He pulled a silken cord by the door, and two serving girls appeared as if from nowhere. They burst into tears of happiness when they saw their mistress standing beside her bed.

"Help the princess with her bath and lay out clothes suitable for the noon meal. Tell the kitchen staff that we will dine in an hour, the princess, I, and these two guests."

"And your friend, Trangaram?"

"Not today," said the prince grimly. "Trangaram will be dining elsewhere for a long time. And send in my bodyguards."

When the bodyguards arrived, the prince instructed them to find Trangaram and bring him to the throne room. They were also to search his house. "Come," he said to Selassie and me, "let us go to the throne room to await my good friend."

We had not been in the throne room long before the guards arrived with Trangaram. He looked perplexed.

"If I may ask, Your Highness, why did you send your bodyguards to escort me here? It is an honor, but I was not aware that I was in any danger."

"Oh, I think you are, my friend," answered the prince. "But more of that later. I brought you here to tell you some good news. Sinbad and his friend have succeeded in their quest. They have returned from

Allepey with the antidote for my wife's unending slumber. She is now awake, never to fall victim to her uncle's wicked schemes again."

Trangaram's face twisted in confusion, but he made a nice recovery. "Why, that's wonderful, wonderful, Your Highness! But, Sinbad, you told me you failed. I don't understand."

The prince held up his hand. "You don't need to answer, Sinbad. The men coming in the door right now will explain your little deception." I turned to see three of the prince's servants enter the room. They held in their hands two scrolls, scrolls that Trangaram recognized.

"Burglars! Sire, your servants have been in my house and have stolen some of my correspondence!" He lunged at the men, seeking to snatch scrolls from their hands before they could give them to the prince, but the bodyguards jerked him back and held him fast. Prince Vishnipim took the scrolls and scanned them

"Well, good friend Trangaram, it seems you are even a better friend of my wife's uncle than of my wife or me. The first scroll is a contract employing you to see to it that the princess would prick her finger on that poisoned rose bush. A pretty sum he promised you, too! And this second scroll expresses the king's appreciation for warning him that Sinbad and Selassie had entered his realm in search of purple zaza fruit. I expect he sent some money with this one."

Trangaram's face was ashen gray. He fell to his knees. "Your Highness, someone planted those scrolls in my house to bring about my ruin. I swear that I was never unfaithful to you!"

"You already admitted that they were your correspondence, traitorous wretch!"

"Please, Your Highness, I beg you, have mercy!"

"I have already decided to be merciful. You shall not die nor be tortured. But I will exile you to Allepey."

"No, lord! The king of Allepey will kill me! He does not suffer failure to remain unpunished."

"Then I will put you on the first ship leaving port, wherever it may go. Return to Ernakulam, and you will die. Guards, see that this traitor leaves on the next boat. Till then, he can enjoy the hospitality of the jailer."

The guards led Trangaram away.

"That was hungry work," the prince said. "The midday meal awaits. For the first time since my dear wife fell into her trance, I look forward to eating. Follow me to the dining hall. There we will talk of the rewards and honors I will bestow on you."

Our first meal with the prince had been sumptuous, but the dinner we enjoyed with him that day was richer still, and far more festive, for his bride was again at his side. She was famished—who wouldn't be after going without food for more than a year?—but as we recounted our adventure with the robbers and the apes, she was so spellbound that she scarcely ate a mouthful.

"I still can't believe that Trangaram was in the pay of my uncle!" the princess exclaimed after we had finished our tale. "And I remember nothing of my slumber. It seems like only yesterday afternoon that I reached out to pluck that golden rose."

"Let's not even think about those things," interrupted the prince. "Let us rather decide what reward would be fitting for you two, who risked your lives for my dear wife and me. Sinbad, Selassie, what can I give you? Whatever you ask, up to half my kingdom, is yours."

"I'll let Selassie speak for himself, Your Highness. As for me, I would be happy with a stout merchantman and a cargo of spices. The spices I will sell in Aden; then I will continue on my pilgrimage to Mecca."

"Your ship and cargo will be at your disposal in three days, Sinbad. And you, Selassie, what will you have?"

"I really don't want anything, except to return to my home in Ethiopia. I will sail with Sinbad. Aden is just a few miles from the Horn of Africa. If I am landed there, I can find my way home. Perhaps a short sword for protection; I don't know what else to ask for."

"Come, come! You must let me give you more than a sword."

"I appreciate your generous heart, Highness, but nothing would give me more happiness than seeing my own land and my family again."

"Why don't you ponder it for three days, till Sinbad's ship is ready to sail? You may think of something you'd like from me."

"Thank you, Highness; I'll do that."

The princess stood up. "I'll leave you men to talk about ships and swords. I must go and set the household in order. After more than a year, I'm sure it needs a woman's touch."

The princess tugged on a silken bell cord, and immediately three servant girls appeared with basins and towels for washing our hands. Two of the maids were Indian, but one was much darker. Upon seeing the servants, Selassie gasped so loudly that the three of us turned round to look at him. His eyes, wider than I had ever seen them, were fixed on the dark girl. At that very moment, she saw Selassie and let out a cry. The basin slipped from her hands and clattered on the marble tiles, but she didn't even notice. As though the prince, the princess, and I were not even there, the two young people began to speak to each other in words I couldn't understand.

Recovering himself after a minute, Selassie turned to us, trembling with excitement. Speaking in Arabic, he said, "Sinbad, this girl is from Axum, my own country! Her name is Maryam, and she is a Christian, like me! She came to Ernakulam with her father four years ago. He came to trade, and for a year, he prospered in his business. Then, three years ago, another merchant paid a high official to bring charges against Maryam's father. He was unjustly imprisoned, leaving Maryam with no money and no one to look after her. She came to the palace seeking a position as a bondservant, for she knew that the prince was a kind and good man. She has been here since. Her father can't get a trial to defend himself against the charges; he's still in prison. And guess who brought the charges? Trangaram!"

The prince flushed with anger, and his brow furrowed deeply. "If I had known that, I would not have spared that dog's life!"

"This is the reward I beg of you, Highness," continued Selassie. "Release Maryam's father. Give him a ship and cargo of spices, like Sinbad. We will all sail together to Aden. From there, Maryam, her father, and I will proceed to Africa and our home, and Sinbad will go on to Mecca—if I cannot persuade him to become a Christian first."

"I am only too glad to grant your request, Selassie," replied Prince Vishnipim. "I wonder how many others are in prison because of the greed and malice of Trangaram!"

When Maryam heard the prince's words, she burst out in tears of happiness. "Thank you, good Prince Vishnipim! I had hoped that someday I would be able to speak to you about my father and plead his case before you. Now God has answered my prayers in a way I didn't expect. And we will be going home, too!"

Maryam wiped her eyes with the towel she had brought in for us; then she and Selassie talked quietly in their own tongue while Prince Vishnipim gave orders to the other servant girls to call the captain of the guard. When the officer came, the prince ordered him to release Maryam's father from prison and to bring him at once to the palace.

I remained silent during this whole exchange of words. Maryam had spoken to Prince Vishnipim in good Arabic, and I could have talked with Selassie and Maryam and congratulated them both. But I felt like an outsider. Certainly, Allah had delivered me from death a dozen times in my life. But I never felt that he did it because I was one of his own people; it was simply an act of impersonal mercy. It seemed that the Maker of all men and women cared for some people like sons and daughters—and they were Christians! This thought didn't depress me; strangely, it excited me! Might I, somehow, become a child of God? Could I do it and remain a Muslim? I didn't see how: The Koran said nothing about becoming a child of God, only a servant. That thought did depress me.

Chapter 16
Gebre's Tale

Two days had passed since our return to Ernakulam. Tomorrow we would sail for Arabia. Selassie and I walked down to the docks to look at the ship Prince Vishnipim had given me. As we threaded our way through the narrow bazaars, Selassie asked me, "Have you talked with Gebre and Maryam, Sinbad? Their story is exceedingly interesting, almost as unusual as the story of your seventh voyage."

"Gebre? Is that Maryam's father?"

"Yes. His full name is Gebre Egziabher, which means "Servant of God" in our tongue. That would be *Abdullah* in Arabic. We Christians do think of ourselves as God's servants as well as his sons. We don't serve as slaves but as children seeking to please their father out of love."

"Interesting indeed, Selassie; I must think on that. To answer your question, no, I haven't had time to talk with them. I've been too busy buying nutmeg, cloves, and cinnamon from the spice merchants. When the prince gives you as much as you want to spend for your cargo, you are like a little boy buying candy with his father's money. But I'd like to get to know them better and hear their story."

When we arrived at the ship, we found a beehive of activity. A line of straining porters struggled up a gangplank, their backs bent over by sacks bulging with spices. The sweating men dropped their burdens on the deck and stiffly shuffled down another gangplank. The crew stowed the cargo in the hold as fast as the porters brought it on board the ship. On the other side of the dock, still more porters were loading a dhow that could have been the twin of mine. That would be Gebre's ship.

We crossed the pier and found Gebre and Maryam there. Like me, Gebre was an experienced trader. He wanted to make sure the crew was securing his cargo well. We were a month into monsoon season now and could expect thunderstorms and pouring rain on the westward voyage. If the spices were not kept perfectly dry, they would swell, then rot.

We hailed Gebre and Maryam, and they turned to greet us. "Good morning, Sinbad and young Selassie," Gebre boomed.

"I'm glad to see you, Selassie," said Maryam with glowing eyes and a warm smile. "And you too, Sinbad," she added hastily. I could tell that Maryam thought a lot of Selassie.

"These crews seem to know their business," I said to Gebre.

"Oh, yes, Sinbad. I handpicked the men myself. They are all old salts who sailed my ship one time or another while I was set up as a trader here, before Trangaram had me thrown in prison. May God be merciful to him and grant him repentance."

"Gebre, Selassie tells me that you and Maryam had quite an adventure on your voyage here from Africa. I would like to hear your story sometime."

"Why not now, Sinbad? Come, let's go have some tea in the bazaar, and I will tell you of the troubles and dangers God delivered us from."

That seemed good to me. Preparations for departure were proceeding well, and we had several hours free before we would take our last meal with the prince and his bride. The four of us pushed through the mass of toiling porters and sailors, then through the crowded bazaar until we arrived at a tea shop. Maryam knew an out-of-the-way rooftop café above the noises and smells of the market. The proprietor greeted us at the top of the whitewashed stairs and showed us to a table with four stools under a bright green parasol. We ordered Darjeeling tea and fresh, succulent mangoes. While we waited for our refreshments, Gebre began his tale.

"Five years ago, a fearful plague swept through Axum; Selassie will remember it. I lost my only brother and his wife, and my wife lost her two sisters and their husbands. Before the scourge had run its course, my dear wife also died. I had already prepared to travel to Malabar to sell our fine Ethiopian coffee and buy spices. All my money was tied up in the ship and cargo. I couldn't back out of the voyage without losing my investment and becoming a poor man. But now that Maryam had no mother and no aunts or uncles to care for her while I was away, what was I to do? My only choice was to bring her with me."

"I was eager to go, Father," interrupted Maryam. "I couldn't bear the thought of being separated from you. Besides, I was afraid that if I remained behind, the plague would return and lay me in the grave also."

"That was another reason for taking you with me," Gebre replied. "Now, let me go on with my story." Maryam pursed her lips and said nothing more.

"Just a month after burying my wife, we closed up the house in Axum and traveled down to Adulis, on the Red Sea, where my ship and cargo lay ready to depart. We set sail on the first of February, and for three weeks, all went well."

"I had never been on one of Father's ships before, and what an adventure it was!" burst out Maryam. "I stood at the railing for hours watching the flying fishes and the seabirds. My sadness left me as I came to realize that my dear mother and my aunts and uncles were now with the Lord. They all knew our Lord Jesus Christ as their Savior from sin and death. He died for our sins, but God raised him from the dead; and he promised to raise those who die believing in him. As Father and I talked about these things, I lost my sadness, even though I still miss my mother so."

"Your mother must have been a very good woman," I said, trying to be polite. "Many women have earned favor with Allah by being faithful wives and mothers."

"Oh, she was wonderful, kind, and good; but her hope of resurrection was not fixed on her own righteousness, Sinbad. Only Jesus Christ was good enough to please God; but he was good on our behalf. My mother was righteous in Christ, as is every true son or daughter of God."

Even this lass, young as she is, knows what she believes, I mused. Like Selassie, Maryam didn't think she could earn God's favor by her own good works but only by the righteousness God simply reckons to everyone who trusts Jesus. At the same time, God enters into a personal relationship with believers and makes them his children. Strange, wonderful ideas! I found myself longing for just what Christians are so confident they have: being a child of God, being right in his sight. Islam didn't promise that.

Gebre took up his tale again.

"For three weeks, all went well. Then one day, just after the midday meal, the lookout sighted a sail off the starboard bow. The sail grew in size as the vessel approached. Much too late to escape, we saw that we were being pursued by pirates!

"The slim, black corsair rapidly closed with our blocky dhow. All too soon, we could make out a score of tough, vicious men crowded against the rail of the corsair. Every one of them brandished a scimitar and had two or three daggers in his sash. As soon as they came within range, the pirates cast grappling hooks into our rigging and drew their ship tight against our port side. My crew tried desperately to slash the lines that held us fast like a spider's web, but there were too many of them. With a roar, the pirates scrambled over the rail and onto the deck of my vessel.

"We were only nine men and had no chance of driving the pirates from the ship, but we could put up a good fight and send some of the pirates to meet their Maker. I had no intention of actually fighting to the death; I was concerned for Maryam above all. I hoped to persuade those brigands to spare our lives in exchange for the lives of those we would surely kill before being overwhelmed. I gave the command to retreat to the poop deck and called for a parley with the pirate chief.

"'Captain!' I shouted. 'How many of you will die before you kill the last of us? Let me make you an offer a reasonable man would not refuse. The ship's boat hangs here at the rear of the poop deck. Allow us to lower it into the sea and row away unmolested. You'll have ship and cargo without any of you being hurt or killed. What more do you want?'

"The captain drew the crew into a huddle, and they talked over our offer. I knew what they were thinking. None of them wanted to die. In fact, they didn't want us to die either: they would prefer to sell us all into slavery. If they accepted my offer, they would have their own lives and the ship and cargo but no slaves. I knew they were plotting how to capture us all without bloodshed, and I was pretty sure I knew how they would try. But I had plans of my own.

"The pirate chief finally rose from the huddle and approached the poop deck. 'We accept your offer. But as a token of your goodwill, you must throw your swords into the sea before you get into the lifeboat. We don't want you rowing back at night, sneaking on board, and killing us all.'

"'No,' I replied, 'we won't lay down our weapons now. To be frank, I don't trust you. But we will throw them into the sea after we have gotten into the boat.'

"'Fair enough,' said the captain, and smiled a wicked grin that revealed yellow, pointed, scraggly teeth.

"Now, while the pirates were scheming how to have the ship and us too, I had whispered instructions to my men. I dispatched one of them to my cabin, where I had sent Maryam when we first realized pirates were after us. If the pirates knew a woman was on board, they might decide to fight anyway, for female slaves fetch a great price in the Zanzibar slave market. My man told Maryam to put on some of my clothes and join us outside; then he gathered up my compass, astrolabe, and charts, stuffed them under his shirt, and brought them out to me. Soon Maryam came out on deck, looking like a cabin boy. My mate sent two other sailors for a cask of water and a chest of bread. All the while, I was aft, talking with the pirates to keep their attention. Miraculously, it seemed to me, the actions of my crew never aroused their suspicions.

"The pirates looked on with sly smiles as my crew lowered the lifeboat into the sea and shinnied down the ropes. Maryam was the last to go, except for me. I kept talking to the pirates, pretending to argue for a better deal from them, hoping to distract them just a little longer. Halfway down, Maryam stopped next to the rudder. In the shadow of the overhanging poop deck, no one above could see what she was doing. Pulling a dagger from her belt, she cut the two lines connecting the rudder to the ship's wheel. Then she let go of the rope and dropped down into the waiting arms of my crew. Last of all, I shinnied down a rope and stepped into the lifeboat

"'Now boys, row for your freedom!' I whispered fiercely. 'Over to the stern of the pirates' ship!' The corsair was lashed to our ship bow to bow, stern to stern. A few vigorous strokes brought us to the rudder of the corsair. We still couldn't be seen from above. The pirates weren't looking astern anyway, for by then, tongues of flame and dense wreaths of smoke were rising from a heap of tarry cordage in the bow of our ship. It was a little diversion I had planned to distract those treacherous brigands. By the time we reached the stern of the corsair, all the pirates were busy trying to put out the fire.

"Unseen, I climbed the rudder till I reached the steering lines, then drew my dagger and sliced them neatly in two, just as Maryam had done to my own ship's gear. Then I clambered up the rudder until I was level with the corsair's lifeboat. I hacked at the lines suspending the boat from the poop deck. One, two, three, four lines parted, and the boat splashed into the green ocean.

"The noise of the boat hitting the water brought the pirates rushing to the stern of my ship, but they could see nothing yet. I hastily shinnied down the rudder of the corsair and got in our boat. 'Half of you climb into the other lifeboat, then all of you pull for it, lads, as hard as you can!' I shouted. My men hauled on their oars with a will, and we quickly drew away from the two ships, still tied fast together by grappling lines. When we were out of range of harpoon and knife, I stood up in our boat.

"'See, Captain, we now throw our weapons over the side, as I promised.' My men were reluctant to part with their knives and swords, but I made them cast them all away. 'They'll do us no good if that band of murderers and thieves catches up with us,' I explained, 'they just make the boats heavier. But don't worry about them now: Look!'

"My men looked back to see the pirates shaking their fists at us as their ship's boat came into view, pulling away from the stern. They realized they couldn't row out and capture us now that we were unarmed, as I knew they were planning to do. The cutthroats rushed to slash the grappling lines that held the two ships together so as to free the corsair for pursuit. What a nasty surprise they had when they hoisted sail and found the rudder wouldn't respond to the helmsman. The pirates left on my ship tried the same tactic and found themselves equally at the mercy of the wind and current.

"The corsair and the dhow were drifting away from each other, with half the pirate crew on the corsair, half on the dhow. It wouldn't take them long to figure out what was wrong, but by the time they fixed the steering, it would be night; already, the shadows were growing long. As we drew away from the two ships, the oaths and curses of the pirates echoed faintly over the water.

"We didn't gloat about how clever we were to escape with our lives. There we were, bobbing up and down gently in the vast, empty ocean, our crowded lifeboats riding low in the water. We raised our voices to God in thanksgiving for his mercy; then we turned to him in supplication, asking him to deliver us from our plight.

"I decided that we would row at night for a few hours to shake off the pirates completely. We could row night or day, for the dark skies were clear, and the starry constellations showed us the way. I had taken a sight of the sun with the astrolabe only six hours earlier, so I knew our latitude pretty well. I would shoot the sun every noon, and we could correct our course as needed. I had both a compass and a chart of the Indian Ocean, so I knew we could find our way home to Africa. The real problem, which I did not tell the crew, was that the chart showed no land within five hundred miles of our location. My hope was to get into a well-traveled sea lane where another ship might pick us up. We rowed till midnight; then we ate and slept.

"'Captain, Captain, look!' A faraway voice penetrated my slumbers. Someone was shaking me and calling my name over and over. I pulled myself to my knees, shook my dreams out of my head, and opened my eyes. It was dawn; the fiery orange sun was already rising over a dark mountain. A mountain! I dipped my hand into the ocean and brought up a handful of salty water, which I splashed on my face. That cleared my head. I rubbed my eyes and looked again. There it was, an island rising out of the ocean, no more than an hour away. By then, everyone was awake. I didn't have to tell them to start rowing; every man already had his oar in the water, rowing as hard as he could.

"Our boats bumped softly on the sandy shore. We all jumped out into ankle-deep surf. 'First things first,' I shouted. 'Let's get these boats above the high tide line.'

"Once the boats were secure, we set off to explore the island. It was a true desert island, bare and rocky. We hoped we might find a pool of rainwater to refill our cask, already a third empty. We set off down the beach toward a cape that jutted out into the surf. Despite the bleakness of the island, my men were in good spirits and sang songs of Axum as they trudged through the sand. Rounding the cape, we came upon a horrifying sight: there in a small cove lay the pirate corsair and my dhow at anchor! On a rocky knoll above the harbor perched a small stone castle: the pirates' lair!

"I frantically motioned to my crew to stop singing and retreat down the beach, but it was too late: we turned around only to find a dozen grim pirates ten paces behind us. They had seen us land and had fallen in silently behind as we marched along the shore. The foremost cutthroat pointed wordlessly with his scimitar at the fortress overlooking the cove. We had no weapons and no choice. We turned around and headed for the castle.

"The pirate chief welcomed us with his wicked, yellow grin. 'I'm certainly glad you decided to accept my hospitality after all,' he mocked. At least he didn't seem angry about our earlier escape. 'My first mate will take you to your rooms. You'll be able to rest there a long time. Then we'll put you back on your ship and sail it to Muscat, where you'll begin a new life.'"

I said nothing as Gebre mentioned Muscat, but I knew what the pirate chief had in mind for his captives. I had purchased Selassie in Muscat. I'd never thought of slaves as real people before I got to know Selassie. The thought of a courageous, intelligent man like Gebre and a sweet, brave girl like Maryam being sold into slavery in Muscat saddened me. I determined that when I made my way back to Baghdad, I would free all my slaves and never buy another.

Maryam interrupted again. "Father, you've talked for several hours already! It's time we were getting back to the palace for our farewell meal with Prince Vishnipim."

"Your daughter's right, Gebre," I reluctantly agreed, "but you can't leave me hanging now. I must hear the end of the story. Perhaps you can finish it after supper."

"Actually, Sinbad, I'll let Maryam finish the story then. She was the one who rescued us all after we were thrown into the pirates' dungeon. And she does like to talk!" he said with a chuckle. "After supper, then!"

Chapter 17
Maryam's Tale

We had said our goodbyes to the prince and princess after a most enjoyable evening, and the four of us were sitting on the deck of my ship, watching the crimson sun begin its plunge into the western ocean. It was a balmy evening, and no one was ready for bed yet.

"Maryam, this would be a good time to tell Sinbad and Selassie how we escaped from the pirates and made our way to India," said Gebre. "As I said before, you're the real heroine of the story."

Maryam blushed and lowered her eyes. "Don't you think you should finish the story, Father?"

"I would really like to hear it from you," exclaimed Selassie. Maryam looked up at him and smiled, her round black eyes sparkling.

"Very well, Selassie, but Father's praise is too generous. As I tell you what happened to us, you will see that God is the one who delivered us.

"The pirate chief ordered his first mate to lock us in the dungeon. A burly pirate grasped each of us tightly by the arm and marched us quick-step down a windowless corridor to the foot of a winding staircase. Down the stairs they dragged us, from one floor to another, all the way to the bottom. There, in the basement of the fortress, the thugs shoved each of us into a cramped cell.

"I admit that I cried bitter tears when that heavy oaken door slammed shut and I heard the key turn in the iron lock. But after a bit, I thought to pray. I asked God to remind me that he was still with me, even there in that gloomy prison, and he gave me faith and peace, strange as that sounds. But then, he promises peace to his people when they commit themselves and their ways to him, peace that passes understanding.

"I looked around my new home. I could see without difficulty, for a high, narrow window let a shaft of blessed sunlight into the room. Our captors had furnished the cell with a cot, a small table, and a stool. I reflected that it could have been worse: I had heard of dungeons where prisoners are chained to the walls and have only straw to sleep on. I ran to the cell door and looked through the small barred opening into the central corridor. A lamp set in a wall sconce gave the only light there. I saw a guard sitting at the foot of the stairs, looking very bored and inattentive. He had no reason to be alert, for no one could escape from those cells.

"The moving shadow on the wall helped me keep track of time. At six in the evening, as well as I could reckon, I heard a key in the lock. The door swung open, and the guard entered the cell. He carried a flagon of water, a loaf of bread, and a cake of dried, pressed figs. He set the food and drink on the table and grunted, 'Here's your evening meal. You'll be fed twice a day.' The man then turned on his heels and left the cell without another word.

"I thanked God for the food, then quickly devoured it all. I hadn't eaten for hours and was famished. I wondered why I was fed so well; then I remembered that the pirates intended to sell us as slaves. They wanted us healthy and fit so as to fetch a good price. In an hour, the cell grew dark as the sun set. I lay down to sleep, and I slept well. God continued to give me peace.

"When I awoke, I found that the sun had already risen. The shadow on the wall told me it was about seven o'clock. Soon the guard came in with my morning ration. I ate slowly this time, wondering if there was any way we could escape from this prison.

"Just as I was about to pop the last morsel of bread in my mouth, a noise at the window startled me. I looked up and saw a magpie on the stone sill, ruffling its feathers and settling down to look at me with beady eyes. I held out the bread in my hand. The magpie cocked its head but remained on the windowsill. Gently, so as not to frighten my visitor, I tossed the crust of bread into a pool of sunlight on the floor. Immediately the bird hopped down and picked it up; then it flew out the window. To my surprise, the magpie returned in ten minutes and deposited a brass button on the floor. Ever since childhood, I had heard the words 'thieving magpie,' but never knew why till that moment.

"'I don't think you deserve such a bad name,' I said to the bird. 'I doubt you took that button off someone's coat; I imagine you found it on the ground. And you are trading it for food.'

"The bird returned the next morning with a silver coin, which it placed carefully on the floor in the sun. I took the coin and gave the magpie a generous hunk of bread. This exchange continued every mealtime for a week. Each time the magpie brought some bright metal trinket to sparkle in the sun, and I gave the bird bread in exchange.

"I had been feeding the magpie for a week when a plan began to form in my mind. The next time the bird came with its offering, I enticed it onto the table with a trail of crumbs. When the bird came within reach, I gently caught it by its feet. At first it was frightened, but I stroked its feathers, spoke softly to it, and fed it a dried fig. My, how that bird liked figs! Soon that magpie was sitting on my finger as tamely as any canary.

"I carried the bird over to the window of the cell and poked its head out through the bars. 'Look over on the guard's table,' I whispered to my feathered friend. 'Do you see that key? Go get it. The guard is napping and won't see you.' I knew the bird couldn't understand me, but I hoped that it would see the key and that its instincts would move it to do what I wanted. God sent ravens to feed the prophet Elijah when he was hiding in the wilderness. Was I foolish to hope that he would move that magpie to get the key and bring it to me?

"The guard's arms lay folded on the table, making a comfortable pillow for his head. He was asleep on the watch, as usual. The bird took off from my window with a single flap of the wings and glided silently down the corridor to the table. It lighted without a sound next to the head of the sleeping guard, picked up the key, and returned to my window as quietly as it left. I put out my finger, and the magpie landed on it. Drawing my hand inside the cell, I took the key from its beak and set that wonderful bird down on the table, where it began to eat all my bread and figs. That wonderful bird had earned its meal.

"I had already thought out what I would do and carried out my plan quickly. I let myself out of my cell, then opened all the other cells and let my father and his men out. Everyone knew that silence was golden; no one made the slightest sound. Father tiptoed up to the guard and gently drew the pirate's dagger from his sash. Then, holding the sharp knife to the man's throat, he awakened the man, showing with signs that the slightest sound would be very unwise! Father's men bound and gagged the guard and put him in a cell. Then Father led us up the stairs and out into the morning sun.

"We had been in near darkness for about two weeks, and at first, the bright light of day was overpowering. But we soon recovered our sight and took our bearings. Both ships still rode at anchor in the cove below. No one was about, for pirates like to sleep late when they're not at work. We made our way down to the water's edge. Three boats had been drawn up on the beach. We got into two of them and rowed out to the pirate's dhow to search for weapons.

"'Snap to, men!' Father barked. 'We don't have time to dawdle. If those brigands discover we've escaped before we can get clean away, we'll have to fight for it.'

"How right he was. Father and his men had scarcely fitted themselves out with scimitars, cutlasses, and dirks from the dhow when we heard cursing and shouting on the shore. There were the pirates, beside themselves with rage. A half-dozen of them piled into the only boat left on the beach and began to row out to us.

"'Well, it's an even match now, men,' declared Father. 'Only half of them were able to get into the boat. Still, I have an idea for getting out of this without bloodshed.' Having said that, Father gave instructions to the crew.

"The pirates reached the dhow and prepared to board it. They were thirsting for a fight. Then Father stepped to the rail and began to taunt them. 'What a miserable excuse for a pirate band you are! Not once, but twice you let us escape right under your noses. What kind of bumpkin do you have for a leader? If he fights as poorly as he leads, even I should be able to best him; I, a merchant who hardly knows which end of a scimitar to hold in my hand.'

"That was too much for the pirate chief, as Father knew it would be. 'Stand aside, boys! I'm going to carve this Ethiopian shopkeeper into little pieces and feed him to the fishes!' roared the captain of the pirates as he leaped over the rail, cutlass swinging.

"I closed my eyes and prayed for Father's safety. I kept my eyes closed and kept praying while the ring of steel against steel echoed and re-echoed over the waters. Clash upon clash, the sounds of the fight ranged back and forth from stem to stern and port to starboard. I had to open my eyes. There was Father, matching the pirate chief blow for blow. Father was grinning as he thrust and parried. The pirate was purple with anger, panting and puffing as he tried vainly to overcome his adversary. Then, with a quick upthrust, Father struck the cutlass from the pirate's hand and backed him at sword point to the rail. All the fight and bluster drained out of the pirate captain like water from a broken jug. He fell to his knees and begged for his life.

"'Tell your men to turn around and row back to shore. Do it now if you want to see the sun go down!'

"The pirate was still gasping for breath, but he managed to rasp out the necessary orders, and his men turned their boat toward the beach. Fear and awe lay upon their faces as they slowly, silently rowed back to their fortress.

"'You'll stay with us till we're well clear of the island,' Father informed his defeated foe. 'Then you can row one of our boats back.' Father put half the crew on our own ship, and in a few minutes, both vessels were under sail. An hour later, when the pirate island was hardly more than a speck on the horizon, Father let the pirate chief row away.

"That's about all there is to tell. We sailed both ships to the Malabar Coast. Father sold the pirate dhow and gave the money to his crew. He then set up as a trader in Ernakulam. You know the rest."

"But your story raises many questions," Selassie said. "Gebre, how were you able to beat the pirate chief so handily, being only a merchant like Sinbad?"

"Come, come, Selassie, you should know the answer to that! Axum is often at war, and most men my age have had to fight for our country. Before I was a merchant, I commanded a brigade of troops for King Menelik. I fought both on the Nubian frontier and in the jungles of the south. Your father is a military man, isn't he?"

"Yes, he is, or was; truly, I do not know if he is dead or alive. But he knew how to fight bravely, and he trusted in God more than his sword. Perhaps the Lord has spared him." Selassie's lip trembled, and his voice quavered as he spoke, though he smiled bravely.

"I will pray that God will spare his life and reunite you again, Selassie; you can count on it," Maryam assured him. "And so will I," added Gebre. "Remember what Jesus promised us: 'If two of you on earth agree about anything you ask for, it will be done for you by my Father in heaven.'"

"Surely Jesus didn't mean God would do anything you Christians want if two of you agree to ask for it!" I exclaimed. "Allah does what he wants, and no one can force his hand."

"True enough, Sinbad," replied Gebre, "But remember, we are his children. God promises good things to his children because he loves us. Of course, Jesus also said he would answer our prayers so as to bring glory to God. An unworthy prayer—say, the prayer of a greedy man for great wealth—is not covered by this promise. But God's children want to glorify him; they don't want to ask selfishly."

There it was again, this Christian belief that they are children of God, in a loving relationship with him. How attractive that sounded! How much I wanted that! But Allah of the Koran was remote and distant.

I changed the subject. "Your daughter's tale prompts me to ask you another question, Gebre. Why did you spare the life of the pirate chief? Why didn't you run him through when you had him pinned against the rail? He robbed you, imprisoned you, would have sold you into slavery, and tried to kill you. You had every right and every reason to slay that evil creature."

"God tells us to love our enemies and to be good to them. Of course, to protect my daughter and my men, I would have done what you suggest if it had been necessary. But God gave me the opportunity to show mercy. After all, I am worthy of death for my sin, but God spared me. It cost me nothing to spare that man's life, but it cost God the death of his Son to spare me. And since Jesus is infinite God as well as true man, the death of that one man could pay for sins against an infinite God, the sins of a multitude of people that cannot be numbered."

"Even the sins of a Muslim like me who has rejected him so long?"

"Yes, Sinbad, if you will repent and believe on the Lord Jesus Christ."

"I, I will think long on what you've said," I stammered. "But it's late, and we need to go to bed now." A smooth, soft voice within told me to sleep on it, that I would be myself, a good, convinced Muslim, in the morning. I wanted to believe that voice, but I knew that a good night's sleep—if I could even get it—wouldn't make my new doubts about Islam or my new longings for a personal relationship with God go away.

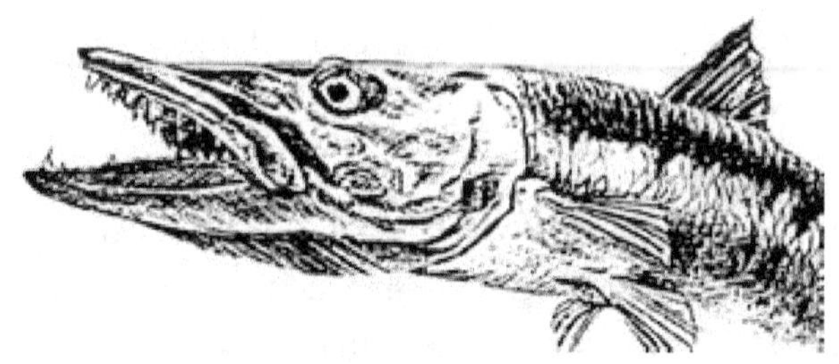

Chapter 18

Homeward Bound!

"Homeward bound!" I rejoiced, as my new ship glided majestically out of the harbor, past the watchtower, past the breakwater, into the open ocean. How I reveled in the cool salt spray on my face and the gentle rise and fall of the deck beneath my feet.

Gebre and Maryam followed in their dhow. Ahead lay a hazy, azure horizon, an uncertain boundary between the cloudless sky and the peacock-green waters of the Indian Ocean. The haze reminded me that masses of humid air billow up from the equator daily during monsoon season. Great thunderheads form every morning only to empty themselves in afternoon downpours on a sea already full to the brim with water. Well, as long as the winds remained tropical breezes, we could live with the rain. The hatch covers were well-fitted, and the scuppers clear of debris; the decks would drain quickly, and the hold would remain dry.

I didn't worry about Gebre. He had made half a dozen voyages from Africa to India and back again during the monsoon; he was an old salt like me. I liked the man. Like Selassie, he was a Christian, but that didn't bother me the way it would have just a few months before. I never knew any Christians personally until I met Selassie. There was a Christian quarter in Baghdad, of course, and I did business with some Christian tradesmen. I had even consulted a Christian physician. But I never wanted Christians as friends. I had been taught that they were blasphemers against Muhammad and the Koran. Now I found them to be as reasonable as other men. They aren't just willful, stubborn resisters of the truth; they have their reasons for rejecting the Koran. I wasn't yet ready to examine those reasons, but I had to admit, grudgingly, to be sure, that Christians aren't pig-headed fools just because they reject Islam.

I turned and looked back over our creamy wake toward the Malabar Coast. Ernakulam had shrunk to a bright, white spot on the emerald shore, a shining pearl on dark-green velvet. Selassie leaned on the rail and stared westward at the sea and sky. We stood together silently for perhaps half an hour. Selassie never looked back at India. His beloved Ethiopia lay less than two thousand miles ahead, and he gazed steadfastly to the west as if hoping to glimpse Africa far across the water.

The first two weeks of our journey were uneventful, even boring. During the day, we fished to pass the time; there was little else to do. On the fifteenth day out, about an hour before the midday meal, Selassie was sitting aft with his line in the water when he felt a sharp tug. He jerked the pole to set the hook and started pulling in his catch, hand over hand.

"Sinbad, come help me pull this fish in. It's too heavy for me; it must be enormous."

I grabbed the line and helped haul Selassie's catch up from the depths. As its head emerged from the waves, I saw that it was a giant sea bass. Together we succeeded in hoisting the finny creature halfway out of the brine, but without the lift provided by the water, we couldn't raise it higher; in fact, the line was in danger of breaking. By now, the whole crew had come forward to watch us. One of the sailors fastened a gaff to a steel cable and managed to hook the fish by the gills. The bass writhed and flailed its tail, trying to shake off the gaff. The sailors made the cable fast to a capstan and began to haul on it as they did when we weighed anchor. Just as the fish cleared the water, an immense indigo wrasse burst forth from the deep in a plume of spray, devoured the bass in one gulp, and plunged back into the sea. Now we had an even bigger fish on the line!

"That critter's bigger than me!" exclaimed Hassan, our cook. "I can feed you on fish for a fortnight if you can land it."

The wrasse was well hooked. We played out the cable and let our quarry run till it tired, then dragged it back to the ship. The creature made a last, desperate run for it. We kept the cable taut and let the fish fight the line; in time, it would tire. In an hour, the cable slackened all at once. The fight had gone out of the brute. Hand over hand, we pulled its limp, spent body back to the ship. We had won.

But no! Before we could hoist the fish out of the water, a third monster, jaws agape, rose straight up from the depths and swallowed the wrasse we had labored so hard to catch. We caught only the briefest glimpse of the creature, but that was enough to reveal that it was indeed a fish and not a shark or whale. But what a fish! I'd never seen its like before. It was as long as the ship's boat. Its shimmering scales were as large and bright as the Caliph's freshly minted silver sequins, and as it gave a careless flip and disappeared under the waves, we could see its tail, wide-spreading as a young palm tree.

The creature started its run. The cable snapped taut, the ship jerked forward, and we began our ride. Our keel cut the surface of the sea like a sharp sword as our clumsy merchant dhow flew through the water. Great arcs of spray shot out to each side of the bow.

The fish pulled us along for an hour and didn't slow down. At first we thought it a great treat to race across the water faster than the dolphins, but then we began to wonder how it would end. What if the beast decided to dive deep into the abyss? It was strong enough to drag the whole ship under! Every man sensed the peril, and each one began to pray. The Hindus prayed to their many gods, and the Muslims prayed to Allah.

I prayed to Allah too, but despair mingled with my fervor. Would Allah heed my plea? He had no particular reason to hear me. I hadn't done everything a good Muslim should do; that was why I set out on my eighth voyage in the first place. The Koran says repeatedly that Allah is merciful; but his mercy is a matter of his will, not his heart. Nothing in the Koran told me that Allah loved me in spite of my sins, as a father loves his child. I was not the child of Allah; I was only one of his creatures, and he had many others.

Selassie also prayed: "Lord God, you sent a great fish to preserve the prophet Jonah. At first he thought it meant his death, but you sent it to save his life. Through his many trials, you brought Jonah to repentance and faith. All of us need to be saved from an ocean grave, but Sinbad needs to be saved from sin and guilt too. Save our lives and save his soul! Give Sinbad saving faith. In Jesus's name, amen."

God didn't answer Selassie's prayer right away. Hour after hour, we sliced through the waves at terrifying speed. Our pace didn't slacken as the sun went down. We saw nothing but heard the most terrifying sounds all night long. Our hull hissed like a venomous serpent as it streaked over the glassy waters; the timbers creaked ominously under the strain. No one could sleep. The men continued to pray to their gods and made the wildest promises to them. One vowed he would become a monk if he were delivered; another promised to bestow all his wealth on the poor; another would go on pilgrimage to Mecca as soon as he reached land safely. Only Selassie slumbered. He awoke several times in the night, but after praying for a few minutes, he would lie back down on his mat and doze off again.

Every morning in the tropics, the sun boils up out of the ocean all at once, like an athlete beginning a race. From the first glimmer of dawn to full daylight is a matter of only a few minutes. I was still rubbing my eyes, squinting in the harsh morning light, when I perceived that we were near land. We were approaching a strange coast that was mostly hidden by a low bank of sea fog. I had no idea where we were. Was it Africa? Persia? Some uncharted island?

The crew were jabbering and pointing at the land. Their excited talk awoke Selassie.

"Where are we, Sinbad?" he asked sleepily.

"I don't know. But wherever we are, we're headed straight for shore." The fish, you see, was swimming straight toward the beach. That was a matter of concern. If the shore was rocky, or a reef of hard, sharp coral lay offshore, we could be shipwrecked and drown just as thoroughly as if the monster plunged to the bottom of the sea, pulling us down with him.

The first mate was a clever man. "Sinbad, cut the cable and let the brute go free," he shouted. "There's no other way to escape."

"You heard Ahmed, boys; cut the cable. And make it quick: we need to cut loose before we're grounded."

The crew went to work with their cutlasses, but they were unable to hack through the steel cable. Finally, Osman, a hulking giant of a man with muscles like thick coils of rope, took an axe to the capstan and hewed it down as he would fall a tree in the forest. The cable, still wound around the severed top of the capstan, went zinging over the rail, scattering wooden splinters and shards in every direction and nearly beheading Mahmud. The fish vaulted forward while the crew was sent sprawling on the deck. They quickly jumped to their feet and let out a cheer: we were saved!

Or were we? We wouldn't be dragged down to an ocean grave, but we were as lost as if we had ridden out a two-week gale without sun or stars to guide us. We had no idea where we were. We hadn't seen Gebre's ship for a day. He would gain Africa without incident—provided he didn't decide to go fishing as we had. I probably would never see him or Maryam again. I wanted to hear more about the Bible and God and Jesus from that wise man, but that was *qismat.*

"I miss them already," said Selassie, who seemed to know what I was thinking. "I hope to see them again. I like Maryam very much. In just the short time I've known her, Maryam has become like a sister to me. And in Christ, she is my sister indeed. Gebre is like an older brother. But you are still my best friend, Sinbad, and I hope someday you will become a brother in Christ too."

"Perhaps Allah will grant you your desire to meet Maryam and Gebre again, Selassie. But now we've got to land on that coast and find some timber to repair the bowsprit."

"What about the bowsprit?" Selassie asked.

"Just look at it," I replied. "The flying cable snapped it off as neatly as anything."

It wasn't impossible to proceed without a bowsprit, only awkward. We rigged the lateen sails as square sails and clumsily drew near to the land. We sailed along the coast for several hours seeking a bay or cove, but we could see very little of the land because of the low-lying fog. I finally decided to anchor a hundred yards offshore and row to the beach in the boat.

I took Selassie and four other men with me to explore the unknown land. I didn't want too many men in the boat, for we didn't want to ride low in the water if we came upon a barrier reef or had to maneuver among rocks. Sure enough, as we approached the shore, we found that a coral reef ran parallel to the coast just inside the fog. We sculled through a shallow channel that meandered between heads of pink and red coral and entered the calm water of a turquoise lagoon. We rowed through the mist, scarcely able to see twenty feet ahead. In a few minutes, we could make out the beach. It looked deserted.

We ran our boat up on the sand and pulled it above the high tide line. Then we set off down the beach to see what we could see. For two hours, we couldn't see anything but the bone-white beach, so thick was the fog around us. I didn't want to go inland till we had a better idea of the lay of the land. The fog would burn off in a little while; then we would know where we were.

By noon the sun had scattered the fog, and we could see clearly. What we saw gladdened our hearts: less than a mile down the beach lay a fishing village.

"Look at that, will you! Let's step lively now!" I ordered. Trudging became trotting, and trotting became running as fast as we could. We arrived breathless but happy at the town square. The inhabitants had seen us coming, and a small crowd stood watching as we approached. They were not Arabs, Persians, or Indians from the look of them; their ebony skin told us that they were Africans.

"These people look Ethiopian to me, Sinbad," said my friend. "But those hills are not the hills of Ethiopia. I'll try talking to that tall character in the center of the crowd. His clothing is old-fashioned, but he looks well-to-do. He could be the chief man of the town."

Selassie greeted the man in Geez. The man replied, and the two fell into spirited conversation. So they were Ethiopians! I was amazed. How did they get here? I didn't know where "here" was, but I knew we were still over a thousand miles from Africa.

Selassie and the man talked for a full hour. What could they be talking about for such a long time? Finally, my friend walked slowly back to us. His face was grave. "Sinbad, I have bad news. The inhabitants of this town are Ethiopians, as are the inhabitants of towns up and down this coast."

"Why, that's good news, Selassie! Surely they're glad to help a fellow countryman."

"Oh, they're quite happy to see me. The bad news is, they told me they intend to make slaves of you and the Arab sailors! They've already sent boats filled with warriors to capture the dhow and the rest of the crew. Look around you!"

I turned to see that we were surrounded by at least fifty men, all armed with a sword at the belt and a long spear in hand.

"Why? Why do they want to enslave us? You did tell them we were your friends, didn't you?"

"Of course! I pleaded for your freedom. I told them how you saved my life and protected me from danger more than once. For that, they agreed not to kill you. You see, they hate Arabs. They've hated Arabs for three hundred years. It's because of Arabs that they're here on this island, cut off from Ethiopia, with no way to return

"We're on a large island midway between India and Africa. This island is unknown in India, Persia, Arabia, or Africa, for it lies well south of the normal shipping lanes. These people have lived here ever since Axum's disastrous wars in Yemen."

"I never heard of those wars. Then again, I know little about Axum."

Selassie filled me in.

"Three hundred years ago, the empire of Axum sent an army across the Red Sea to conquer Yemen. Axum easily overcame the Yemenis and began to settle our people there alongside the native population. The Yemenis didn't welcome Axum, and many fled north into Arabia. A generation later, Axum was troubled by rebellion all over the empire. Taking advantage of our weakness, Yemenis and Arabs attacked out of the desert and overwhelmed the distracted forces of Axum. Our emperor sent a new army into Yemen, but it was poorly led and suffered a disastrous defeat.

"The victorious Arabs enslaved the Axumite settlers and killed most of the soldiers. Some of my people managed to escape on ships from Aden just as the monsoon season began. Now, we are not naturally a seafaring people. The ships tried to stay together, but the winds and waves dispersed the little fleet. One ship was driven far out to sea and ran aground on this island. From that pitiful band of refugees have descended the inhabitants of this coast. They blame the Arabs for all their misfortunes."

"It seems to me that the Axumites began the whole affair by invading Yemen and conquering the people there."

"Oh, that's very true. I'm not defending what Axum did. We Ethiopians are supposed to be a Christian nation, but many who think they are Christians don't have a living faith in Christ. Without Christ, we can be as greedy and overbearing as any people. But rightly or wrongly, Sinbad, that's why they intend to enslave you and all the Arabs in the crew. They have no quarrel with the Hindus. They're going to send them away in the ship."

"Why don't they take the ship and sail back to Ethiopia themselves? I'd gladly guide them in exchange for my freedom."

"They'd need a whole fleet of ships. But, Sinbad, there is a way to avoid slavery. I proposed a plan to them. If you accept the plan, they won't sell you into slavery; in fact, we'll be able to continue our voyage to Africa."

"I'll agree to anything, Selassie. What is your plan?"

"I told them how you're a seafaring man who has sailed the Indian Ocean many times. I promised that you would show them how to build a fleet of ships so that the whole population could return to Axum. You'll train them in seamanship and then guide the fleet. They promise to let you go when they reach the Red Sea. Frankly, I don't trust them: I suspect they intend to sell you when they get there. These men may be my countrymen, but they thirst for revenge. Still, you're a clever man. I'm sure you'll come up with a way to avoid any treachery."

I'd been in tight spots before and faced dangers aplenty but never undeserved hatred. Why had Allah allowed this to happen to me?

Chapter 19

The Deadly Viper

"So what exactly is a Negus, Selassie?" I asked as we walked down the road.

"*Negus* is our word for "king." The leader of these exiles can't really be a king since there's only one Negus, and he rules in Axum. But when the refugees settled here, they appointed one of the generals to be the Negus of the colony. The current Negus is the eighth in his line."

Now I knew where we were going. Two soldiers were bringing us to the only real city in the country to see the Negus. The townsmen who captured us thought Selassie's proposal would please their king. We were about to find out if they were right.

When we arrived at the city, we went directly to the palace. The guards conducted us to a long, vaulted room. At the other end of the room was a dais with a high-backed throne that was painted a brilliant green, red, and yellow. On the throne sat a tall, slender man with a regal bearing—obviously the Negus. On either side stood a stocky warrior with his arms crossed on his chest, a short sword in each hand.

The Negus beckoned Selassie to approach the throne. He seemed not to notice me at all. Selassie drew near and gave a slight bow. The Negus spoke to him in Geez, and Selassie replied. They talked for a quarter hour or so. Then the Negus stood up and made a gesture with his hand, which I recognized as a dismissal. Selassie bowed again. The Negus stepped down from the dais and departed through a side door, flanked by his bodyguards. We were left to find our own way out.

"Well, what did he say?" I asked impatiently once we were back on the street. "Since I seem to be at liberty, they must have accepted the deal."

"Oh, it's even better than that," replied my friend with a smile. "You don't have to build a fleet large enough to take all the exiles back to Axum. The Negus is quite happy ruling his own island. He has no desire to return to a land neither his father nor his grandfather ever knew. But he does want to trade with the mother country. There's no gold on the island—you noticed that the throne was painted, not gilded, didn't you? And you must have taken note of his feather headdress. In all the land, there is no gold to make a proper crown. But there are apes, ebony, and spices that he would like to trade for gold.

"The Negus requires only five ocean-going dhows. Since yours rides at anchor offshore, that leaves only four to build. I told the Negus that it was your pleasure to make a gift of your dhow and all its contents to him as a token of your respect. It was an empty gesture, I know, since your ship is in his possession anyway; but the man is quite vain, and I think it pleased him."

Before I could question Selassie further, the guards who had escorted us to the palace appeared and led us to the bungalow where we were to stay while the fleet was being built. When we arrived, we found the rest of the crew, both Arabs and Hindus, waiting there. I explained the situation to them. Their part would be to train the most intelligent, daring, and fit Axumites in the arts of seamanship.

Very early the next morning, before the tropic sun burst forth to run its race, I awoke to a thump, thump, thump. Someone was pounding on the door of our sleeping quarters. Selassie went to see who it was and returned to inform me that two dozen husky men with axes and saws awaited us in the street. The Negus was enthusiastic about Selassie's proposal and wanted to begin that very morning.

"These men will take us to the center of the island, to the forest. There, you are to direct them as they cut the timber they'll need for the ships." Rubbing the sleep from my eyes, I dressed and washed and told the crew what was up. Then Selassie and I departed with the woodcutters.

The hills that rolled down to the coast were bare and rocky. As we plodded up one switchback after another, the sun glared down from above and reflected off the white limestone cliffs. Neither shade nor water was to be found. By noon we were tired, thirsty, and covered with fine chalky dust. Fortunately, the Negus had provided each man with a full skin of water, as well as bread and dates.

The sun was two hours past the zenith when we finally stood panting at the top of the pass and gazed through red-rimmed eyes at a green and gold plateau. Tall grass stretched out before us, dotted with reed-lined waterholes. Beyond the grassland lay a dense forest. We rested a bit, then pushed on to the edge of the woods, where we made camp beside a deep, clear pool.

The next morning, we went into the forest with the men. The trees of that country were known to me, and I was able to tell the men just what they needed to cut: so many logs of such and such a tree, so many of another kind. After talking with the foreman, Selassie informed me that we could return to the city. "We're not needed here now," he announced. "The Negus wants you to return so that you can organize the sail makers and oversee their training." That was fine with me. The sooner we could sail for Africa, the better.

The trip back to the city would be mostly downhill, and I expected to be back before sunset. We set off at a brisk pace. Selassie led the way, and with the exuberance of youth, he was soon out of sight. We were deep in the tall grass, not far from the top of the bluff, when I heard Selassie cry out ahead of me, "Sinbad, come quickly!"

I ran forward and found my friend sitting in the middle of the trail. He was holding his foot. "Sinbad, this snake bit me!" I looked down and saw an emerald-green viper still clinging to Selassie's foot. I grabbed the snake by the tail and gave it a shake. The hideous thing released its grip, and I quickly crushed its head with my heel before it could coil and strike again.

Selassie's foot didn't look good. An angry red patch spread out from two neat puncture wounds on the top of the foot, which was already beginning to swell up. "I'm getting dizzy, Sinbad, and my foot feels like a lump of ice. Now my leg is getting cold." My friend was shivering, even though it was the heat of the day

A deadly venom was working its way up Selassie's leg. My friend needed the help of a skilled physician right away. I picked him up and began to push my way desperately through the grass toward the edge of the plateau. I made good time, but by the time I started down the rocky hillside, Selassie was already unconscious. I stumbled and slid down the switchbacks, racing against time.

Miraculously—it had to be a miracle—I reached the bottom of the mountain trail without falling. I ran all the way to the city, straight to the palace of the Negus. One glance at Selassie's foot told the guards what had happened, and one of them ran off to find help. He returned with a bearded old man in tow. He had to be the royal physician.

The man gently touched Selassie's foot, felt his forehead, and took his pulse. Then he looked at me with tears in his eyes and shook his head. He had no cure. The old man gently laid Selassie on a couch in the guards' vestibule and covered him with a thin blanket to give him a little warmth. Again he shook his head sadly and departed.

I rushed out of the palace into the city square. Up and down the square, I paced in despair. I couldn't do anything for my friend. The royal physician couldn't do anything either. Selassie would die, and we were powerless to prevent it.

I wept till I had no more tears left. Then I lifted my face to heaven and prayed:

"Jesus, I have always thought of you as a prophet, just a great man of God. But if you are also truly God, as Selassie says, you can hear my prayer. Selassie tells me you healed many people when you were on earth. Won't you heal him now?"

I hurried back to the palace to see if Jesus had healed Selassie right then. My friend still lay on the couch. He was hardly breathing now. I felt his brow. It was burning, yet he was shivering and shaking. I rushed out of the palace again. I jammed my hands down in my pockets and walked up and down, beside myself with hopelessness and grief. The fingers of my right hand closed on a small cylinder deep in the pocket, and I drew it out and looked at it; I don't know why. It was the flask of zaza juice that awakened the princess. My eyes, red with weeping, stopped crying as a flame of hope sprang up in my breast.

I bounded up the palace steps two at a time, pushed the guards aside, and ran to Selassie's side. Kneeling down, I uncorked the vial of purple elixir. I forced open Selassie's mouth and shook three drops onto his tongue. Then I sat back on my heels and waited.

I didn't have to wait long. Within minutes, my friend stopped shivering and began to breathe more deeply and rhythmically. He seemed only asleep now, not feverish. I felt his brow and let out a sigh of relief. It was cool again. I pulled back the blanket and looked at the poisoned foot. It was still puffed up, but only half the size it had been just ten minutes before, and the dark red patch around the bite had faded to pink and shrunk to the size of a fig.

I remained by Selassie's side all night, but I was no longer anxious. Danger had passed; my friend would get well. As I sat there, I wondered: Did Jesus answer my prayer? Was it the elixir that healed Selassie, or did Jesus do a miracle? If it was the juice, would I have found it anyway, or did Jesus bring the bottle into my hand?

Just as golden dawn flooded through the lattices and made curly shadows on the limestone floor, Selassie stretched his arms, opened his eyes, and yawned. "Sinbad, what am I doing here?" he inquired with surprise. I ordered tea and cakes, and while a servant went to fetch them, I told Selassie everything that happened. "I don't know if Jesus answered my prayer or if I was just lucky in finding that vial of elixir," I concluded.

"Oh, Jesus did it, Sinbad, one way or another," affirmed my friend. "God usually uses means, like the zaza juice, but he has healed many miraculously, without means. The Bible tells us that. When Jesus was on earth, he once healed a blind man by putting mud on his eyes and telling him to go wash. It wasn't the mud that cured the man's blindness, but Jesus did it that way so the man could exercise his faith."

"Well, I don't have your kind of faith in Jesus; at least, I don't think so. I don't know why I prayed to him, though. Why didn't I just bury my head in my hands in despair?"

"I hope it's because God has given you a mustard seed of faith and that the seed is growing. Oh, may it grow into saving faith! Sinbad, you must let me read you stories from the Bible, stories of Jesus healing the sick and afflicted."

"You know we Muslims honor Jesus as a prophet of Allah, Selassie. But the Koran doesn't tell us much about what he did or said. I'd like to know more of the things Jesus did and taught—when we have time," I hastily added. "There's no hurry. I don't want you to think I'm ready to become a Christian; I'm just curious, that's all."

In saying this, I was trying to convince myself more than Selassie. I already knew, deep in my heart, that Jesus was far greater than I used to think. Muslims think Muhammad was the greatest of the prophets.

But he never healed anyone. Jesus had healed Selassie; that I knew beyond a shadow of a doubt.

In a few days, Selassie was as good as new. By then, the harbor was full of activity. Carpenters were busy day and night sawing logs into planks and spars, trying to keep up with the shipwrights as they fitted together the keels, ribs, and planking of the four dhows the Negus required. Sail makers were hard at work producing not only sails but also cargo nets and miles and miles of rope. I had to instruct them in all their duties, for the Axumites had never built any craft larger than a coastal fishing boat.

Selassie served as my interpreter. Day after day, while all this was going on, the servants of the Negus brought spices, hides, ivory, and caged animals into the capital from all over the colony. My sailors spent hours without number training all the local fishermen as well as a picked company of the Negus's servants in the ways of ocean seamanship. It's one thing to go fishing a mile or two from shore when the weather is fine; it's something very different to sail on the billowing green ocean with only the sun and stars to guide, riding out typhoons when the monsoon blows up out of the west.

At last, three months to the day from the morning we dropped anchor off the coast of this unknown land, the fleet was ready to sail. The dhows, laden with rich cargoes, rode low in the water, and the Axumite sailors stood at attention on deck for final inspection by my old crewmen, now their new comrades. Speaking through Selassie, the Negus said goodbye to me:

"You have kept your end of the bargain, Sinbad, and I am keeping mine. Lead the fleet to Adulis, the great port of Axum. I've placed soldiers on your ship to ensure that you don't decide to go your own way. When you reach Adulis, my soldiers will board the other ships, and you will be free to go anywhere you please in your own ship with the cargo you brought from India. You see, I give you back what is your own, the ship and cargo you so graciously gave to me."

I thanked the Negus, and he returned to the palace while I boarded my ship and gave orders to set sail. As the crews raised the sails and they puffed out in the morning breeze, I reflected on the king's last words. Fairly spoken they were, but could I trust them? Selassie had told me he thought the Negus intended to have all the Arabs sold for slaves. The presence of soldiers on my ship suggested that my friend was right. I had over a month to come up with a plan to foil that scheme. It didn't seem like much time.

Chapter 20

From Frying Pan to Fire

At first, our voyage went well. The Axumite sailors handled the dhows expertly, the winds blew steadily from the southeast, and God blessed us with a westerly current. I used an astrolabe to determine latitude, but of course, I had no means of determining longitude. We would sail by dead reckoning: north to the latitude of the Red Sea, then due west till we reached it, however far that might be. At the latest, I calculated, we should sight the Bab al-Mandab in six weeks. That meant I had plenty of time to come up with a plan to escape the Negus's treachery if Selassie's hunch was right.

As things turned out, I had much more than six weeks to think, though my mind was occupied with other matters. Fifteen days after weighing anchor, the wind died without a moan, and the sails went slack. We were becalmed. All that day we floated motionless on the glassy sea, and all the next day, and the next. This is my fault, I mused; what was I thinking? In sailing north, the fleet had sailed right into the doldrums, those latitudes where the breezes fail for months at a time. Only the monsoon relieves the stillness of the air, and the monsoon would not blow up for at least three months. The current continued to bear us slowly westward, but at the rate we were drifting, we would run out of food and water long before we reached Africa.

Ahmed commanded the dhow nearest mine. I signaled for him to row over to my ship for a conference. As soon as he was on deck, I came to the point:

"Ahmed, we're in a tight spot. We're becalmed in the doldrums. We'll die of thirst before we reach land if we just sit here bobbing up and down like corks. I have an idea. It's a slim chance, but slim is better than nothing. We're going to harness the lifeboats to the dhows and tow them out of the doldrums. We'll go through the food and water faster, laboring like that, but it's a risk we have to take. If we row for a week, maybe two weeks, we may find breezes farther north. I think the men can strain at the oars that long before they're too weak to row any more. If you have a better idea, tell me; but we must do something."

"This would be a good time to catch another monster fish and let him take us for a ride, but that's not going to happen," Ahmed joked grimly. "I agree: your plan is our only hope."

We rowed over to the other dhows to tell their captains the plan. I solemnly ordered them not to tell the Ethiopians any more than necessary. "If they know how desperate our situation is, they may panic or turn on us in fury and despair. Just announce that this will get us to Adulis faster. And give every man a double ration of food and water today."

So began a two-week ordeal such as I had never undergone before or since. We toiled at the oars day and night. Every man took his turn, officers as well as men. We all rowed a day shift and a night shift. Even Selassie pulled an oar for a half hour each day. The cool night shift was tolerable, just an hour of hard labor, but the days were brutal. The glaring ocean was as bright and hot as an iron grill on a fire of dry thorns. The Arabs blistered and peeled as the sun's rays beat down on them. Even the ebony skin of the Ethiopians wrinkled and cracked under the merciless sun. An hour at the oars was all a man could take. The rest of us had to lift the rowers out of the boat at the end of their shift, so little strength did they have left. We would lay the exhausted men in the shade of the deck awning and force a cup of water down each throat. After a few minutes, the men would be able to sit up, but most of them couldn't rise to their feet for at least an hour after their fiery trial. When they were able to walk around, they would take a little food and more water.

"Will this ever end?" one of the Arabs asked me. "Don't you think hell must be like this, burning hot and never-ending?"

"By my reckoning, we should be out of the doldrums in two or three days," I replied. I wasn't entirely truthful with the man. We might encounter breezes in two or three days, but perhaps we would never catch them, for the current was beginning to turn south. I knew it would turn south as it neared Africa, and you might think I would have rejoiced to think that Africa was near. But by turning south, the current would carry us back into the heart of the doldrums. In fact, we were already pulling against the current. So far, we were winning; but if a breeze didn't pick up in a few days, and if the current turned even more, we would never escape from the doldrums.

The sailor's remark about hell disturbed me. I had put spiritual concerns out of my mind during our pull for life, but all the anxieties that moved me to go on pilgrimage in the first place flooded back into my mind. Was I good enough to please Allah? I tried so hard—or did I? Selassie's words came back to me: no one is righteous, not one. Nothing we do can tilt the balance in our favor, for a perfectly holy God demands perfection. That's not what we Muslims believed. We are taught that Allah weighs our good deeds against our bad and that if we are good enough—not perfect, but good enough—Allah will admit us to paradise. But I never knew what "good enough" was, and I knew I wasn't perfect.

Selassie freely admitted that he wasn't perfect either, but he had no fear of hell. He believed that Jesus was perfectly good in his place and that Jesus suffered and paid for his people's sins. Well, if Jesus went through worse pains than those we suffered out there in the broiling sun, he suffered greatly indeed! The more I thought about it, the more frightening hell became to me. It had to be infinitely worse than our agony in the sun. I had to find out if Islam was really true or if Selassie was right. The stakes were too high to be less than sure.

Night fell, and after my turn at the oars, I lay down to sleep. That was a waste of time. I tossed and turned on the hard deck as I wrestled with thoughts of sin, righteousness, and judgment. When it was clear that I wasn't going to get any sleep, I got up and walked around on deck. I looked out at the dark, empty sea. Four lanterns twinkled in the blackness, marking the positions of the other dhows. As I stared into the night, my hands suddenly gripped the rail. A line of faint lights gleamed far away. Ships? Land? What could those lights mean?

One of the sailors saw them, too, and excitedly woke the others. Before long, we all crowded the rail, staring at the mysterious lights across the water. The oars lay idle in the empty boat; no one was rowing as everyone waited silently to see what dawn would reveal.

Dawn came on with a rush and, with it, the cry of the watchman: "Land ho!" Yes, we could all see it now, yet another uncharted island rising from the ocean. I'd come on more than my share of such islands in my long career at sea, but every one was a welcome haven, and this island especially so. Its jade-green slopes told me that it was wooded; and a wooded island would have water and fruit, maybe goats and deer, too. We wouldn't die of hunger or thirst after all!

I didn't need to give any orders. Tired as they were, the sailors piled into the boats and began to pull on the oars with renewed hope and vigor. Everyone wanted to row now. Four men handled the oars in each boat. By the time the sun grew warm, we were inside the reef. Before us lay a small bay ringed by a beach of black volcanic sand. A flashing silver stream tumbled down the green mountain slopes and discharged into the bay. Graceful terns flew low over the turquoise waters seeking fish; scarlet parrots perched in the trees at the edge of the sand. After what we had been through, it seemed we had sailed into paradise.

We dropped anchor and prepared to go ashore. "Drink your fill, and eat all the fruit you want, but keep an eye out for the inhabitants of this place. Those lights mean that someone lives here. The islanders may be peaceful, but it pays to be cautious. Carry your knives, but keep them out of sight under your clothes. If you meet anyone, be friendly but be on the watch. Before you do anything else, fill the water casks and bring them back to the ship; also look for fruit. And keep your eyes open for wild game. Roast venison would be a feast right now; goat would be fine, too. Make sure the ships are provisioned before you go off exploring. If the islanders prove hostile, we'll have to make a quick getaway, but at least we'll have food and water to keep us till the monsoon arrives."

I decided to remain on board till the crew had restocked our supply of food and water, and I kept Selassie with me. The Axumites left two guards to keep us company. Since the men could neither understand us nor speak with us, it was clear that they were there to keep an eye on me. I spoke my mind to Selassie.

"Your countrymen really must plan to sell me into slavery. They don't leave me alone for a minute, not even here."

"I'm more certain of it every day, Sinbad," agreed Selassie. "I hear them talking sometimes when they don't know I'm around. I also hear you talking sometimes when you don't think I'm around. I heard Ali ask you about hell. You didn't really answer his question."

"We Muslims believe hell will be a burning place with scorching winds. Ali knows that as well as I do. He didn't expect an answer; he was only commenting on how beastly hot it was."

"We Christians believe the same about hell. The Bible also describes it as outer darkness where men weep and gnash their teeth. Sinbad, I don't want you to go there! Let me read the Scriptures to you. There we learn how to avoid that place of torment."

"I told you, I'm willing now to hear you read from your Book. We Muslims do recognize it as the Word of God, you know. The first free moment we have, you can read your Bible to me. This evening, after supper, if you like."

This time I wasn't putting my friend off. I did want to hear from his Book. But events would delay the reading. As I was assuring Selassie that I would listen to the Bible, we were roused by a shout from shore. It was Ahmed.

"Help, Sinbad! We've found the inhabitants of the island, or rather, they've found us. Soldiers in strange uniforms surrounded us as we swam in a forest pool. The others were taken prisoner; only I escaped."

As we looked on in horror, armed men burst forth from the trees and seized Ahmed. They dragged him away.

"Sinbad, what's to prevent those men from rowing out to the dhows and capturing us, too?" asked my friend in alarm.

"Nothing. If we stay here, that's just what they'll do. The best thing is to go ashore and hide in the woods. We've got to find the crew and rescue them."

"In Axum, we have an old proverb, Sinbad: 'From frying pan to fire.' It sounds like that's what we'll be doing if we row ashore. They're bound to find us."

"The woods provide much more room to hide than the ship," I replied. "Besides, the crew are my responsibility. And don't forget that the two of us can't sail this dhow alone, especially when the wind comes up. If we don't rescue them, we'll never get home."

"You're right, of course," my friend agreed. "I guess I was just afraid."

"What, afraid? You claim that God is your Father and that he is always with you. How can you be afraid?"

"Oh, we Christians know what it is to be afraid. We don't always keep the Lord before us, as we ought to do. But God brings us back to our right minds and drives us to our knees to seek his presence and help. The Bible contains some wonderful songs and poems, called psalms. In many of them, King David pours out his heart to God with all its fears. He pleads with God for peace and for deliverance from all his dangers. And he praises God for answering his pleas. David was a man after God's own heart, and I want nothing more than to be a man after God's heart too. I'm learning to lay my fears before God and to trust him. Do Muslims believe that God comes alongside to help them become better Muslims?"

"Well, no; that's up to us. We're told to be good Muslims. We're told what we must do to become good Muslims. But Allah doesn't help us become better. Come now, we don't have time to talk about this. We've got to get ashore and hide before the soldiers return and take over the ship."

Leaving our two guards napping in the shade of the poop deck, we got into the remaining ship's boat and rowed to the beach as fast as we could. When the boat bumped the sand, we jumped out and ran into the woods. Not a minute too soon! Looking back through the trees, we saw a platoon of soldiers marching along the shore toward the boats. The soldiers climbed into three of the boats and began to row out to the dhows.

"They didn't see us, Sinbad, or they would have sent a squad to flush us out of the bushes."

"That gives us time to find a good hiding place. Let's go."

We hadn't gone far before we stumbled onto a rough animal trail. It wound around large trees and boulders until it ran up against a steep bluff. We hurried along the base of the bluff, tripping over roots and stumbling over mossy rocks, until Selassie stopped and pointed up. About twenty feet above us, a mat of vines hung down the stony bank.

"Sinbad, look at how the parrots dart in and out of that green drapery. There must be a cave behind it."

Selassie scrambled up the bluff with the help of the vines and peered into the mass of tangled greenery. "Just as I said, Sinbad! Come on up." With that, he disappeared behind the leafy curtain. I followed him up the crumbling stone bank. Soon we were sitting in the perfect hiding place. The parrots squawked angrily at first but quickly came to tolerate our presence and settled down.

We looked out through the tangled vines on the scene below. We couldn't see very far, but we could hear well. In the distance, we heard the soldiers muttering and cursing as they returned empty-handed to the beach. They soon guessed that we had fled to the island and began to search for us. One patrol after another passed below us, but the few who looked up never saw behind the vines that concealed us from view, and none of those who did glance upward thought to climb up and take a look behind the green curtain.

After a few hours, we didn't see or hear the soldiers anymore. They must have gone inland. The cave was roomy enough to lie down in, so we decided to nap till nightfall and then go in search of our friends.

Selassie withdrew to the back of the cave to pray for a few minutes, as he always did before retiring. I should have prayed also. Muslims are supposed to pray five times a day, but to tell you the truth, I had ceased to pray some weeks before. Too many things about Islam were not right. How I wished it were light enough in the cave for Selassie to read his Bible to me. The dimness of the cave impressed on me how in my life I was walking in just such darkness.

Chapter 21

A Bride for Sinbad

Selassie's voice roused me from a fitful slumber. "Wake up, Sinbad. It's getting dark. Time to explore the island." I sat up, rubbed the sleep from my eyes, and peered through the vines that concealed our hiding place. Dusk was falling fast. My stomach felt as hollow as a dried gourd. I wished Selassie had awakened me earlier so that we might have looked for some food before setting off in search of my men.

"I woke up an hour ago, Sinbad, and I was famished, so I went looking for something to eat. I found a mango tree. Here, try some of these; they're ripe and succulent."

Thanking my friend, I ate a juicy orange mango and put another in my sash. "Let's go," I whispered.

We jumped down from our cave—straight into the hands of a dozen waiting soldiers! With hand motions that could not be misunderstood, they indicated that we were to go with them. Off we started, surrounded by armed men. Escape was impossible.

"Sinbad, this is my fault. These men must have seen me gathering fruit and followed me back to the cave."

"Don't blame yourself, Selassie. I think they knew all the time that we were in the cave. Why should they skin their knees and soil their uniforms climbing up that rocky bank when they knew we'd come down eventually?"

The soldiers marched us along the bluff until we came to a wider trail. The trail became a road; the road became a paved highway. Whoever the inhabitants of the island were, they were civilized. In little more than an hour, we arrived at a city. The stout stone walls and crisp lines of its buildings shone softly in the moonlight. The soldiers took us to their barracks. They put us in separate rooms and indicated with signs that they would return in the morning.

My room was not a cell but more like a room in an inn. It contained a bed, a table, and a chair. On the table sat a pitcher of water and a cup. I took a sip of water and surveyed my quarters. The bed looked comfortable enough, and the bedclothes were clean. I tried the door and found it unlocked. I could walk out any time I wanted, but that would be pointless—where would I go? Were we prisoners or guests? Where was my crew? I stretched out on the bed, hands behind my head, and pondered these questions.

I had scarcely begun to ponder when an orderly brought in a tray of fruit, cheese, rolls, and a cup of sweet jasmine tea. He set the tray on the table, bowed with a smile, and left. As I ate and drank, I wondered why I was being treated so well. The soldiers who met us at the beach had dealt roughly with us—why the change?

The soldier returned with a basin of hot water, soap, and a soft towel. He cleared away the remains of breakfast while I refreshed myself. Then the man gestured that I should follow him. Out in the hallway stood another soldier. Selassie was by his side. As we trailed after our keepers, I asked my friend how the guards treated him.

"Very well indeed, Sinbad. I felt more like a guest than a prisoner. The way the soldiers hunted us down and hauled us away, I expected to sleep on flea-ridden straw and to be fed only bread and water. This is all very puzzling."

The guards led us out of the barracks and through the streets of the city to the other side of town. The clothing of the residents was like nothing I had ever seen. Both men and women wore knee-length tunics featuring green, scarlet, and canary yellow stripes; under their tunics, they wore black or white trousers. No one except the soldiers wore any sort of head covering. They weren't dressed like Arabs, nor like the Axumite Ethiopians. What kind of people lived here?

We arrived at an imposing villa situated in the middle of a park. The soldiers brought us into a richly decorated reception hall, clicked their heels, and left us there alone. We looked around. Embroidered tapestries depicting hideous mythical beasts hung from the stone walls. A knotted carpet of bizarre design covered the tile floor. To our left, a disgusting idol leered at us from an alcove in the wall. Across the room from the idol was an arch fitted with an intricately carved and painted door. Like the creatures rampant on the tapestries, the revolting figures on the door pictured creeping things and foul birds that never lived in this world. How ugly is idolatry, I reflected.

As we gawked at the outlandish furnishings surrounding us, the door to our right swung open, and a short, portly man in a robe of silken brocade waddled into the room. A beautiful young woman, also richly dressed, and an older man in Arab dress followed him. The lady looked at me, smiled, and whispered something to the fat man.

"Welcome, Sinbad," said the old man in Arabic. "My name is Gamal. I am the interpreter for Lord Orglu and his daughter, Lady Orglu. You are their guests."

I bowed low. "Tell the lord and lady that I appreciate their hospitality. But I have many questions. How do you know who I am? Where are the crewmen of my ships? Why did the soldiers treat us so roughly at first? And how did you, an Arab, come to be here in this place and among this people unknown to Muslims, Christians, or Hindus?"

"Patience," Gamal chuckled, "I'll answer all your questions. As for myself, I was a fisherman in Zanzibar until a great and sudden storm carried me hundreds of leagues east and cast me ashore on this island, naked and more dead than alive. That was thirty years ago. The people of the land befriended me. I learned their language and now serve as an adviser to Lord Orglu, the governor of this part of the island.

"As for the men who came with you, I've been quizzing them all night; that's how I learned who you are. I told Lord Orglu about you and your seven voyages, and he had you brought here."

"Why did the king's soldiers treat us so roughly at first and so kindly later?"

"We thought you might be a war party. This island is not entirely unknown to the outside world. That's why we have an army. Once we learned who you were, your men received kind treatment."

I felt much better. "Now that you know we're only peaceful merchants on our way to Africa, I would beg a favor of Lord Orglu. Let us remain here till the breezes freshen and we can continue on our journey home."

"That is why Lord Orglu summoned you here. He is willing to grant your request, provided that you do one thing in return."

"Whatever you say! What is it?"

"Lady Orglu has yet to find a suitable husband. She is, as you see, strikingly beautiful and has no lack of suitors. But my mistress finds them all dull and uninteresting. When I told my master and mistress about your exploits and adventures, her eyes sparkled with delight. She asked that you be brought here so that she could meet you. I can tell you that she is pleased with your looks and bearing."

I had a bad feeling about the direction Gamal was heading with this speech.

"So, Sinbad, just now, the young lady asked her father to obtain you as a husband for her. Lord Orglu is an indulgent father; he granted her wish. My master is pleased to give you Lady Orglu's hand in marriage and a rich dowry with it. After the marriage ceremony, you and your bride will settle down here for the rest of your lives. The rest of your expedition may depart after that whenever the winds turn favorable."

I was speechless with shock and confusion. Lady Orglu was beautiful, in a proud, cold way, but I felt nothing for her. Even if I had, I could never marry a *kafir*, an unbeliever. While I struggled for words to decline graciously, Gamal spoke rapidly to Lord and Lady Orglu. After they conversed in their throaty, barbarous tongue for a few minutes, Gamal turned to me. "I told my master and mistress that you were speechless with delight at the prospect of marrying Lady Orglu. After all, you really have no choice."

"What do you mean?" I asked with a sinking heart.

"Since I announced that you agreed to marry my mistress, if you were to reject the lady now, it would be an insult meriting instant, painful death, a death your friends would all share. Come, come, Sinbad! You are a very lucky man! Shall we set the ceremony for tomorrow?"

I needed time to think. "Gamal, I'm really quite ill. Tell your master I need a few days to recover from our ordeal at sea. When I'm well, we can set a date." Gamal offered my excuse to Lord Orglu, and he nodded to indicate that a short delay would be acceptable. Gamal spoke again to the guards, and they escorted us back to the barracks.

"Sinbad, we're in a real fix," said my friend when we were finally alone. "I see plainly that you have no desire to marry that young woman. I completely agree, but that puts all our lives in jeopardy. But what am I thinking? You are Sinbad, the man who escapes time and again from danger. I imagine you've already concocted a scheme to deliver yourself and the rest of us from this predicament."

"I don't have a plan yet, Selassie. I need time to think. It may take more than wits to come out on top. I could just marry the lady, of course. She's beautiful and rich, and life here would be as comfortable as life in Baghdad. And the rest of you would be able to sail on to Africa without me. I wouldn't be sold into slavery either; there's that.

But I can't marry a *kafir*. Besides, I would lose you, my best friend. Who would read to me from the Bible? I'm determined to hear what the Bible has to say. I must know if Islam or the Christian faith is the true Way.

"Dear friend, please pray that God will deliver me from this marriage and all of us from this island. You say that God loves his children like a father. Surely your God will listen to the prayers of his child."

"God doesn't always give us what we ask for, Sinbad."

"Do you say that because I'm not good enough for God's favor?"

"Oh, no, that's not what I'm saying. It's true, of course, that no one is good enough, neither Muslim nor Christian. God hears the pleas of his people because they come to him through Jesus. We pray in Jesus's name, and Jesus brings our prayers before his Father."

"Well then, why don't you just start praying in the name of your Jesus that God will transport us across the sea, you and your countrymen to Adulis, and me and the other Arabs to Jiddah?"

"I'm not going to tell God what to do, Sinbad. I'll ask him to deliver you from marriage to Lady Orglu, and I know he'll answer that prayer somehow. As you said, to marry an idolater would be a sin, and God tells us in his Word that he'll always make us a way of escape from sin. I'll ask God to send us on our way to Africa, too. These things I will pray for, but I'm not going to tell God how I think he should bring them about."

"But does he intend good for me and all the rest of the non-Christians in our party?"

"The Bible tells us that God is good to all his creatures. I believe he intends good for you even though you're not a Christian. Yet." With those words, Selassie retired to his room. As I sat on my bed and tried to think, the Geez language sounded faintly in my ears. On the other side of the wall, Selassie was praying for me.

Chapter 22

Darkness at Midday

I wasn't able to delay the wedding long enough to come up with a plan. Lord Orglu insisted that it take place on the new moon. According to his heathen priest, that was the luckiest day of the month for beginnings. What an unlucky superstition for me: that gave me but two days!

The first night I lay awake from dusk to dawn, trying to hatch a plan. Nothing. I tossed and turned; I got out of bed and paced back and forth in my room. Nothing. I threw myself down on the bed and racked my brain again. Still nothing. Morning finally dawned. I dragged myself out of bed, too tired to think but not too tired to despair. My stomach was tied up in knots, and I ate nothing all day. I used to pride myself on being clever in a tight spot, but this time I hadn't a clue what to do.

The next night, the night before the wedding, was no better. My brain was frozen. I couldn't think to save my life. Although I was weary, I couldn't enjoy even a brief hour of blessed, forgetful sleep. Lying in bed, I gazed out the window as the progress of the constellations marked the passage of the nighttime hours. On a normal night, the stars seem hardly to move at all, but that night they were in a rush, swiftly rising and setting before my anxious eyes. Morning and the dreaded wedding were striding deliberately, rapidly toward me.

Near dawn, I fell into a troubled sleep and began to dream. In my dream, I was standing with Lady Orglu before the heathen priest. He was reciting some mumbo jumbo I couldn't understand, but I understood all too well that I was being married to Lady Orglu and could do nothing to stop it.

But wait! Before the priest finished his ritual, a great roc, that rare and speckled bird, reached down from the sky and snatched me away. The roc carried me to the harbor and deposited me on the deck of my ship. No sooner had the giant bird departed than a whirlwind swept down from the hills above the city and filled my sails, propelling me swiftly out of the harbor. I looked astern and saw my other ships following. Behind them, Lord Orglu's corsairs were in pursuit. The whirlwind continued to speed my ships along, but lo! Behind us, it changed into a waterspout that overwhelmed and capsized Lord Orglu's fleet. We were saved! I let out a cheer—and woke myself up.

"Only a dream, it was only a dream," I murmured to myself. As I looked around my room, soft sunlight filtered through the window lattice, and the song of birds floated on the air. Nature was happy, but my heart was wrapped in black gloom. There was no escape from this marriage save the death that would instantly follow my refusal.

The Lord's attendants served me breakfast and dressed me in a silver gown. Then they escorted me to the palace. Four guards in dress uniform surrounded me. Were they an honor guard for the groom, or did Lord Orglu sense my reluctance and intend to make sure I went through with the ceremony?

When we arrived at the palace, everyone else was already there. Selassie, the Axumites, and my sailors were seated with the guests. The priest stood on a dais at the head of the great hall beneath a hideous, grinning idol. The guards brought me to the priest and motioned for me to turn around to face the assembled witnesses.

As soon as I turned around, trumpets blared from the back of the hall, and Lord Orglu appeared in the doorway with his daughter on his arm. Step, glide, step, glide, on came my bride and her father as a battery of giant drums kept up a deep roll: *brrum*, *brrum*, *brrum*. When the lord and lady arrived at the dais, the guards signaled that I should turn around so that all three of us were facing the priest. The drums stopped all at once, and utter silence lay over the hall like a suffocating blanket.

The priest began to read aloud out of a little book, just as in my dream. But there would be no roc to snatch me from danger this time. I knew Selassie had prayed for my deliverance, but this time his prayers had failed to move his Jesus. I hadn't prayed at all; I simply had no faith that Allah intended to deliver me. The darkness was closing in.

The darkness *was* closing in: the room itself was growing dark! The priest choked on a few words, then stopped reading and let the book slip to the ground as fear and awe clutched at his throat. Voices in the crowd began to moan and cry out. Lord Orglu turned white and started trembling; Lady Orglu fainted dead away. The whole assembly was on the brink of panic.

But I was not afraid. My mind cleared like the morning mist. I knew right away what was happening and saw in an instant my way of escape. Of course! Today one of those rarest of celestial events had begun, a solar eclipse. The moon was passing in front of the sun, darkening the sky. Eclipses of the sun happen only at the exact hour the new moon begins. And that was precisely the scheduled time for the wedding.

I sprang up on the dais and called for Selassie. He bounded forward. "Quick as you can, find Gamal and bring him here. I see my way now."

Selassie was back in a moment with the old man. He had the presence of mind to bring a lamp, too. Falling silent, the crowd turned and gazed at the thin flame as though it were the only light left in the world. Fear still filled every heart, but for the moment, that little lamp kept fear from turning into hysteria.

"Gamal, interpret well my words," I commanded. "If you fail me, this crowd will panic and trample us all in a rush for the doors. Tell them that darkness has fallen because the one true God is angry that I am being forced to marry a pagan. Tell them to let us depart in our ships; then the sun will return. Make Lord Orglu swear in front of the whole crowd that he will do this."

Gamal turned to his master and delivered my message in a voice loud enough for all the guests to hear plainly. Even if he wanted to refuse, Lord Orglu wouldn't dare to do so for fear of his people, for they were terrified by darkness in mid-morning. But no one was more frightened than Lord Orglu himself, and he readily consented to our departure. In fact, he indicated with frantic gestures that we should all leave instantly. The people themselves picked us up and carried us down to the harbor, so heartily did they want us gone.

By the time we arrived shipside, the sun was emerging from its hiding place behind the moon. I spoke again to Gamal: "Admonish Lord Orglu and the people not to detain or pursue us, or a far worse thing will happen." The old man turned around and repeated my warning to the crowds. He must have embellished my words, for they all screamed, turned on their heels, and ran pell-mell back into the city. Not a man remained.

"Well, men, let's weigh anchor and sail away before their fear subsides and they think to come after us." The men fell to work with a will, and we were back on the high seas before the sun crossed the noon meridian.

After the noon meal, Selassie and I talked about our unexpected deliverance.

"Jesus answered my prayers, Sinbad. What do you say to that?"

"Not so fast, Selassie. I am grateful to Allah that I got out of there without having to marry that *kafir* woman, but the eclipse was going to happen whether or not you prayed. I'm grateful for your concern for me, and your prayers too, but why should I believe that Jesus sent the eclipse in answer to your prayers? It wasn't exactly a miracle."

"Remember what I told you before," Selassie replied. "God doesn't always use miracles to perform his will. Most of the time, he uses ordinary means. But ordinary means are in his hand as well as extraordinary ones. Think about this: What if Lord Orglu had set the wedding for a different day? What if today had proved to be an ordinary new moon? Most new moons don't have eclipses of the sun, you know. What if Lord Orglu hadn't provisioned the ships with food and water beforehand but had waited till after the wedding? What if the people of the island had known about eclipses? Then they wouldn't have panicked so. What if you'd been too tongue-tied to seize the opportunity? You couldn't think clearly before the eclipse; you told me that yourself. What if you'd devised some harebrained scheme that backfired? You've never been at a loss for plans and schemes before, but this time your mind stayed blank for days. Miracle or not, our escape was planned and directed by God."

My friend was right, and I knew it. Jesus was to be thanked for our deliverance. He had to be more than a prophet. You don't pray to prophets—I would never think of praying to Muhammad.

"Selassie, I have to admit that you're right. Please, read about Jesus to me from your Bible. I have to know who the real Jesus is. How about tonight, after supper?"

"With great joy, Sinbad! And do you know, this answers another of my prayers to Jesus. I've been praying for months that you would want to know him. Tonight then."

Chapter 23

Betrayed!

A fresh breeze from the southeast billowed our sails as the fleet sailed into the afternoon sun. The doldrum season was over; we were on our way home. In a few hours, Selassie would read to me from the Bible about Jesus. That's what I thought as I rowed over to the chief Axumite's ship after the midday meal. I wanted to confer with him about cargoes and currents.

I'd learned a little Geez, and the Axumite leader had learned a little Arabic; with the help of gestures, we made the needed arrangements without too much difficulty. The chief bid me farewell and retired to his cabin as I prepared to row back to my own ship. The waves seemed a bit choppy, so I decided to stay on the Axumite ship for a while, hoping for quieter seas later in the day. I found a shady spot behind the water casks, lay down, and promptly fell asleep.

The murmur of voices awakened me. One of the Hindu sailors was talking to the Axumite chief. They communicated in very simple Arabic, and what they said awakened my worst fears:

"Are there enough of us to overpower the Arabs before we reach Adulis?" asked the Hindu.

"If you Indians join us, we can easily subdue them," the Axumite replied.

"I've made sure of all of our men," the Hindu said. "You can count on us. After all, we've got a lot to gain from this: bigger shares of the cargo for every man, to say nothing of the silver sequins we'll receive from the slave merchants. But what about Sinbad's friend, Selassie? He may be an Ethiopian like you, but I think he's loyal to Sinbad."

"You're right," the Axumite agreed. "He would lay down his life for his friend. We haven't breathed a word of our plans to him. He'd spill the beans as soon as he heard the news. Not much he can do about it, though, once we've sold the Arabs into slavery."

"He can pray," laughed the Indian.

"He ought to give thanks that the ancient defeat of his own countrymen by the Arabs will finally be avenged," said the chief savagely. "But Selassie takes religion more seriously than the rest of us. Christians are supposed to forgive their enemies, but we on the island have nursed our grudges for three hundred years. Revenge is what we thirst for; the money we'll get when we sell the Arabs as slaves matters little."

I lay on the deck behind the casks, barely a yard from those traitors, hardly daring to breathe.

"When do we make our move?" asked the Indian.

"After we pass through the Bab al-Mandab. I'm not confident my men can navigate in the open ocean if trouble blows up. After all, this is their first voyage. We may still need the skill of the Arab sailors. But after we leave Aden and enter the Red Sea, we ought to be able to follow the coast to Adulis without difficulty."

"I should think so! Sailing on the Red Sea is practically like sailing on a pond. And you have us Indians to help."

The voices faded away. I peeked over the edge of the barrels. The plotters were nowhere in sight. I scurried across the deck, climbed down the rope ladder to my boat, and rowed back to my ship as fast as I could.

What was I to do? The Axumites and Hindus outnumbered the Arabs on every one of the ships except Ahmed's. When the moment for the uprising arrived, the traitors would seize all the ships at once. My first thought was to warn Selassie of the plot, but I thought better of it. I didn't think he could keep a secret. Selassie would instantly go to the Axumite chief and tell him his Christian duty. That would reveal that I knew their plans, and they would clap us in irons then and there.

While I was pondering what to do, Selassie showed up, Bible in hand. "Would you like to hear about Jesus now, Sinbad?"

"Something's come up that I have to deal with right now, Selassie. I'll have to hear you tomorrow."

My friend's face fell, but he went away, saying nothing. I went forward to the bow, where I could be alone to think. An Axumite sailor was standing watch, gazing westward into the night as if to catch first sight of the land of his fathers. I relieved him of duty and sat there alone, deep in thought. Once again, I had to use my wits to get out of a tight spot. But this time, my mind was not a blank. By the time the red star Antares had risen in the east, I knew what I would do.

My plan was simple and sure. I'd row over to Ahmed's ship and fill him in about the plot. His crew, which was nearly all Arab, would force the Hindus and Axumites into the lifeboats. Then we would simply sail away from the rest of the fleet by night. The others wouldn't discover we were missing till dawn, for we had anchored for the night, and they were fast asleep. (The Axumites refused to sail in the dark, even with Arab and Hindu sailors manning the ships.) By morning, we'd be out of sight. Sailing day and night, with our superior seamanship, we'd reach Aden well before the Axumites. I'd tell the sheikh of Aden, a personal friend of mine, everything that happened, and he would arrest the Axumites and Indians when they arrived.

The only bad part of my plan was that I'd have to leave Selassie behind. He'd be safe, of course, for he was an Ethiopian, and the Axumites would never harm him. But what if the Axumites didn't go to Aden? What if they landed at Djibouti instead? Then I'd never see Selassie again. And I'd never hear what the Bible had to say about Jesus. But I could see no other way to avoid being sold into slavery. I had to take the risk.

I decided to leave a letter for Selassie. I would tell him my plan and ask him to meet me in Aden. I returned to my cabin and wrote:

> Selassie, my best friend,
>
> By the time you read this letter, I will be many miles from you. I discovered today that the Axumites have conspired with the Indians to sell all the Arabs into slavery when we reach Adulis, just as you warned me. We are sailing to Aden, where my friend the sheikh will be waiting to seize the traitors when you arrive. Don't worry about me. Pray to Jesus for me. You did that before, and I'm sure Jesus heard your prayers. I do want to learn about him, but it seems we'll have to wait till all this is settled.
>
> Your friend, Sinbad

I left the cabin and searched the deck till I found Selassie asleep on a bale of raw silk. I slipped the letter into his Bible. I took a good look at my friend. He slept peacefully. It seemed to me that Selassie always slept peacefully. Was it just the deep slumber of youth, or did Allah answer his evening prayers by dispersing all care? I resolved to ask him this, too, when we met again.

I sought out the half-dozen Arabs on my ship one by one as they lay sleeping on the deck and, in urgent whispers, told them of our danger and my plan. We silently let the largest boat over the side and rowed to Ahmed's ship. I climbed to the deck and tiptoed to the captain's cabin while the others waited in the boat. Ahmed was still awake, studying the Koran by candlelight. He almost cried out with surprise when I slipped into the cabin, but I had my finger to my lips, and he understood that something secret was up. I told him of the treachery of the Axumites and Indians and of my plan. He agreed at once and went to waken his Arab sailors while I went to the rail and motioned for my men to climb silently aboard.

When all our men were armed and ready for action, Ahmed woke the Axumites and Hindus and roughly ordered them into the boats.

"Your fellow traitors over in the other ships are dreaming away. No doubt they're already counting the money they expect to get from selling us. You'll have to wake them gently and tell them the bad news that half of us have sailed away for Basra." Our destination wasn't really Basra, of course, but the Hindus knew Basra was my homeport, and Ahmed thought to deceive them as to our destination.

Ahmed didn't have to tell them twice to quit the ship. Half asleep but fully afraid for their lives, the confused Axumites and Hindus scrambled down the rope ladder into the boats and made for the other ships, paddling as fast as they could with their hands: we had removed the oars, for we wanted plenty of time to get away. We hauled up the sea anchors, hoisted sail, and set a course by the stars for the northwest.

We sailed day and night for two weeks as we strove to reach Aden well ahead of the other ships. I should have been satisfied with my state: the winds were exceptionally favorable, I had a cargo below decks that would make me wealthy again, and I was bound for Arabia, where I could finally complete my pilgrimage.

But I had lost all interest in the pilgrimage. I was now convinced that becoming a *Hajji* would not make me more acceptable in the eyes of Allah. When I left Baghdad, I thought I was almost good enough to please Allah. Now I knew better. Why, if the eclipse hadn't cut the wedding short, I believe I would have married Lady Orglu after all, *kafir* though she was. It was all very fine to imagine I would have refused to marry an idol-worshipping heathen and gone manfully to my death, but I was so afraid as I stood before the priest that I would have submitted meekly to the marriage. If Allah looked on the heart, I was done for.

Allah is merciful and compassionate, the Koran said. But his compassion is for those who obey and submit to him, not for sinners. And Allah is so distant, so remote from men. The God of the Koran had no personal interest in me. Why should he? I was a creature of his, not a son. A Muslim doesn't pray to Allah as a father the way Selassie calls on the God of the Bible as his father. Selassie! How I missed my friend. Well, I would see him in Aden before long.

The cry of "Land ho!" interrupted my breakfast the twenty-second day after we made our escape. I hurried out on deck, and my heart swelled with happiness as I saw the gray mountains of the south Yemen coast and the bone-white city of Aden at their feet, just an hour away over the waters.

"Ahmed! Have you been in Aden before? Do you know where the India docks are?"

"Of course, Sinbad! I've been in Aden at least a dozen times. Leave it to me; I'll sail us right up to the India docks. Why don't you go below deck and prepare a present for your friend, the sheikh, as you said you would?"

The sheikh of Aden was my friend, but it had been some years since I'd last seen him. I wanted to make sure of his favor by giving him a generous portion of the choicest spices in the cargo. I made up a basket of cinnamon, cloves, and nutmeg—just a personal gift from his old friend Sinbad. I regretted that all the ivory and ebony were in the other ships, but I'd be sure to give him presents of those when I recovered my ships. I draped a cloth of finest Indian silk over the sweet-smelling basket, climbed back on deck—and walked straight into the arms of Osman and Omar, two of my trusted Arab sailors! With a grin, they snatched the basket from me and expertly clapped cold iron fetters on my ankles and hard manacles on my wrists.

"What's the meaning of this? What do you think you're doing?"

"Just carrying out Captain Ahmed's orders, Sinbad. He doesn't want any trouble from you. It might upset the other slaves."

I wheeled around and saw, to my horror, that we were not at the India docks after all. We were at the slave docks. Ahmed, my trusted lieutenant, had betrayed me.

Chapter 24
Sinbad, the Slave

"The more I thought about it, Sinbad, the smarter the Negus's idea sounded to me. Only, I get to be the seller rather than the one sold. The crew and I will get a bigger share of the cargo this way as well as whatever price you fetch in the slave market." Ahmed took pleasure in explaining the roots of his betrayal as his men hustled me through the dockyard on the way to the slave market.

"After all I've done for you!" I exclaimed. The depth of Ahmed's treachery overwhelmed me, and I couldn't find words to say more.

"Well, you did get us out of a couple of messes, but you also got us into them; I guess that's even."

I recovered myself enough to ask in desperation, "How could you do this to a fellow Muslim? The Axumites have no love for us; I can see how they could plot to sell me. But we Muslims are supposed to be a brotherhood!"

"Come, come, Sinbad! I daresay Muslim slaves are keeping your house clean and swept even as we speak, awaiting your return from pilgrimage." I had no answer to that. I again vowed silently to myself that if I ever got home safe and sound, I would free all my slaves at once.

What an evil institution slavery is, I realized! I'd never really thought about slavery before, when I was the master. But now the shoe—or the fetter—was on the other foot. I saw for the first time how wicked it is to treat another human being as a personal possession. If man was made in the image of God, as Selassie's Bible says, and if Jesus died to make men free, as his Bible also says, then the Christian religion is at its heart an enemy of slavery. Islam, on the other hand, matter-of-factly accepts human bondage and approves of it.

My musing ended when we reached the slave market. Ahmed made the rounds of all the slave traders, seeking the best price for me. Some slavers had no interest in a man my age: "I only buy slaves under twenty years of age," said one grizzled merchant. "I specialize in brawny slaves that can carry heavy burdens," said another. "This man looks healthy, but he's too wiry for me." "Can he cook or wait at table?" inquired another. "Cooks and stewards are my line. Could I interest you in a cook for your ship?"

Ahmed was patient and finally found a slave merchant willing to pay a decent price for me, thirty silver sequins. The two men shook hands, and the slaver counted out the coins. Ahmed handed me over to the merchant's personal bodyguard, a hulking monster who could crush me with one huge paw if I tried anything clever.

The brute jerked my chain, practically pulling my arm from its socket. I lurched forward in tongue-gnawing pain and followed the merchant's man across the great open expanse of the slave market, trotting to keep up so the chain would hang loose and my throbbing arm would not be stretched to the breaking point again.

When we arrived at the merchant's warehouse, the guard pushed me into a large room with a half-dozen other slaves. He slammed the massive iron door and turned the key in the lock. Here I would remain till market day. Through the barred windows, I could see the bright blue sky filled with terns and gulls wheeling over the harbor. They were free, but I was not.

I turned to my fellow unfortunates, and we introduced ourselves to each other. All were adult males. Two were Africans, one was a Frank from the West, and the other three were Arabs like me. The Africans were *kafirs*, the Frank was a Christian, and the Arabs were, naturally, Muslims. All had been captured in various wars except for the Frank and me, and all had been sailors. I learned from my companions that our owner was a Persian who specialized in slaves for seafaring merchants: sailors, sea cooks, and cargo handlers.

"How does this Persian treat his human merchandise?" I asked them.

"Oh, he feeds us well and takes us for a walk along the seashore every day—in chains, of course. The man doesn't want us to grow pale and flabby inside this dark holding tank. He wants us in tip-top shape on market day."

"I've got to talk to him. This is a big mistake; I'm no slave."

The Frank guffawed. "You mean, you weren't born a slave. Neither was I. I was a baron in Burgundy before I decided to seek greater glory fighting for Prester John against the Muslims."

"Prester John?" I asked, puzzled.

The Frank continued. "In Europe, many believe there exists a Christian kingdom in the east ruled by one Prester John. Some believe his kingdom to be in Africa, some in Asia. While on pilgrimage in Jerusalem, I asked about Prester John. An Egyptian merchant told me that he ruled in Ethiopia and invited me to accompany him on his return to Egypt. From there, he said, I could follow the Nile upstream to Ethiopia. But when we reached Egypt, that wicked man sold me into slavery!

"I wasn't born a slave, but I am one now," the man concluded. "Each of these men will tell you the same thing: we were all born free. Our master has heard that tale of woe hundreds of times. He's never released a slave out of pity for his sad history. You can try to talk your way into freedom, but you might as well save your breath."

I was sobered by the Frank's words, but felt I had nothing to lose. So when the slave merchant came into the warehouse to inspect us the morning of market day, I put on a big, friendly smile and addressed the man: "Sir, I need to speak with you. There's been a big mistake. I don't belong here. I'm not a slave at all; I'm Sinbad the Sailor. You've heard of me, I expect?"

"I've heard of Sinbad the Sailor, yes; but how do I know that you are that famous man?"

"Why, you can ask the sheikh of Aden himself. We're good friends. If you bring me to his palace, he can vouch for my identity."

"Is that so? Then I'll make quite sure that you come nowhere near the palace. You're a healthy, intelligent man with a good command of Arabic. You're bound to fetch a good price. If there's the slightest chance that what you say is true, I don't want to lose my investment in you by showing you to the sheikh.

"But if the sheikh finds out that you've sold his friend, you'll be in big trouble."

"That's not going to happen. For one thing, the sheikh isn't in the city today. He's across the Red Sea on a state visit to Djibouti and won't return for a week. By then, you'll be leagues away on some outward bound dhow.

"But . . ."

The merchant cut me off before I could plead further. "Listen, Sinbad—if that's who you really are—your words fall on deaf ears when they fall on mine. Any more talk like this, and I'm likely to get angry. I've been patient with you, but your next owner may not be. I suggest you don't argue with him about your state. What you were is of no consequence; you're my property now. I paid good money for you. In just a few hours, someone else will pay good money for you, and you'll be his property."

"You're forgetting something," I shot back in anger. "Someday, I can buy my way out of slavery. When I do, I'll see to it that my friend the sheikh punishes you severely."

"Your threat is idle, Sinbad. There's been a lot of thievery by slaves of late. It seems they're always trying to amass enough money to purchase their freedom. To put a stop to it, all the sheikhs and emirs of Arabia issued a common law this year: no slave may purchase his own freedom at any price, nor may a man free his slave. Slavery is perpetual in these parts. You'll never come back as a free man to take revenge."

"But I may be sold into another country, where I can buy my freedom."

"If I sell you to a foreigner, it will be to one who has no love for Arabs. Such a master will never set you free. Abandon any hope of liberty, Sinbad. You'll be a slave till you die."

With those words, the hard-hearted man turned and left the room. "Follow him," said the chief guard, gesturing with the handle of a large whip. We followed our owner out of our dim quarters into the hot, bright sun. Buyers and sellers filled the street, but the crowds parted quickly to make way for us, as though we were unclean lepers. We made our way single file down a short street to the slave market.

A score of stalls filled the plaza. Each stall consisted of a large awning furnished with a stool and a small table. On the table lay scales for weighing money. Our master led us to his place of business, took his seat, and ordered us to sit on the ground under the awning. The guards took their place on either side of the master. All was ready. The man was open for business, awaiting the customers who would bargain for our bodies.

I sat slumping, my head bowed in despair. It wasn't just that I was being sold into slavery. I'd been in worse spots before. I knew I'd eventually find a way to escape, even if I couldn't buy my freedom. But this time, I couldn't forget my many conversations with Selassie. The root of my despair was that I was enslaved by sin, and I couldn't escape or buy my way out of that. Once I thought I could. I had confessed Allah as God and Muhammad as his prophet; I prayed five times daily, fasted during Ramadan, read the Koran, gave generous alms, abstained from pork and wine; and now I was going on pilgrimage. All these, I thought, will go in the balance on one side to outweigh my sins on the other side on the Day of Judgment.

But seeing the scales on the master's table made me think. I saw clearly now what I had only seen dimly before. I couldn't pay for my soul with good deeds any more than I could pay for my body with silver. The sheikh's law didn't permit the one; God's law didn't permit the other. Slaves couldn't buy their own freedom, and I was a slave of sin. A foreigner could purchase my body and set me free if he chose to do so, but who could purchase my soul from sin?

The harsh voice of the slave merchant shattered my meditation: "Sinbad, stand up. A customer wants to get a look at you, just the kind of foreign merchant I should like to sell you to." I rose to my feet and stepped into the glaring midday sun. At first, I was blinded and could make out nothing, but as my blinking eyes adjusted to the light, I saw the man who might be my next master. His ebony skin told me at once he was an Ethiopian. I studied his face. I knew this man: Gebre!

Chapter 25
Sinbad, Child of God

Gebre! Before I could blurt out a word, Gebre warned me in simple Geez, "Give no sign that you know me."

"I'm sorry, sir; I didn't understand your last remark," said the slaver.

"I was speaking to this slave. It would be a bonus if the man knew Geez, our language."

"I wish I could tell you he did, but you see that he didn't respond to you. I happen to know that he hails from Baghdad. I doubt he speaks anything but Arabic. But he's a very intelligent man and an experienced sailor. Normally I wouldn't take less than one hundred silver sequins for an old salt like him, but I like your looks. I'll let you have him for ninety sequins, though I'm hardly making any profit at that price."

Gebre was used to bargaining. "That's much too high. Look at those gray hairs. I'll wager his teeth are worn. You there, show me your teeth." I obediently opened my mouth wide.

"Just look at them! I'm not some rube from Nubia; I'm from Axum, and we know our slaves. Still, there must be a few years of useful work left in him. I'll give you forty sequins."

"Forty sequins? What do you mean, forty-five sequins? I wouldn't think of letting him go for a paltry fifty sequins. But I do want to expand my business with the men of Axum, so I'll take a loss and let you have him for seventy-five."

So it went, back and forth. Both men were patient, experienced hagglers. Eventually, they settled on a price of sixty sequins. Gebre paid the man and led me away.

When we were out of sight of the slave market, Gebre turned to me with a smile.

"You freed me from prison in Ernakulam, Sinbad; now I've returned the favor. It's good to see you again! When your ship leaped forward and raced away from the rest of the fleet, we didn't know what to make of it. We furled our sails and rode at anchor for a day and a night. When it was clear you weren't going to return, we continued on our way to Adulis. You'll have to tell me what happened when we get back to my ship."

"And you'll have to tell me what brought you to the slave market in Aden at just the right time," I replied. "You weren't going to stop at Aden, if I remember your plans; and you told me yourself that you had no slaves nor ever wanted them."

"Here we are at the dock, Sinbad. The answer to your question is waiting for you on my dhow."

I raised my eyes to the ship's rail and saw Selassie and Maryam looking back at me, broad smiles on their faces. I bounded up the gangplank and hugged my friend. Tears of happiness ran down to my beard.

"Selassie! So you told Gebre that I would be in Aden. But how did you know I was to be found at the slave market? And how did you get here before I did? I was sure our dhow was days ahead of the others."

"Last things first, Sinbad!" chuckled my friend. "We had wonderful winds, the best I've ever had in my short life at sea. We got to Aden in half the time you said we would when we set sail. You must have been too far north or south to catch those miraculous breezes. I think that's what they were, miraculous. God wanted me to get here before you, and I did.

"I asked my fellow Axumites to drop me off in Aden. Of course, they wondered if I knew anything about your escape and if we had arranged to meet here. But inquiries revealed that you hadn't arrived, so they just left me and sailed on. They're probably in Adulis by now. I went to the Ethiopian quarter to find lodging, and who should I find but Gebre and Maryam! Gebre was having his dhow repaired. He and Maryam also had their adventures and delays on the way home."

"I'm eager to hear their story," I replied.

Selassie continued: "When I told them you were making for Aden too, they informed me you hadn't arrived yet. We decided to wait for you. I sat on the sea wall all day, every day, looking out on the great, green, rolling Indian Ocean, scanning the horizon for your familiar sail. Finally, I arrived at my watch one morning to find your ship already riding at anchor in the harbor.

"But before I could board her to greet you, here comes Ahmed with his crew, leading you by a chain like a dog. I followed at a distance and saw them sell you to Ghotzebed the Persian. I ran back to tell Gebre. You know the rest."

Gebre showed me to a cabin where I washed, shaved, and put on fresh clothes. Then I lay down for a short nap. When I awoke, I felt like my old self again.

We had supper in a seaside café. Over roast lamb, saffron rice, and a savory vegetable medley, Gebre asked me about my plans. "Sinbad, I freely give you half of the profits from my cargo. With them, you can continue on your pilgrimage if that is what you still intend to do."

"I've changed my plans, Gebre. I no longer believe the *hajj* will make me more acceptable to Allah. I've come to realize—no, better to say that God has made me realize—that I'm a slave to sin. I want to be free from sin; I want to be a child of God. Islam doesn't offer that. Islam offers a prophet, Muhammad, and a book, the Koran. But the Koran promises paradise to those whose deeds are good enough to please God. There's no hope for me there.

"Selassie tells me that your faith offers Jesus, who is more than a prophet, and a book, the Bible, that tells about Jesus. Can Jesus make me free from sin? Can he make me acceptable in God's sight? Can he make me a son of God? What does the Bible say about that? What hope does the Bible give me? I am hungry to hear it now."

Gebre's face glowed as he replied, "Selassie has a Bible with him, Sinbad. Suppose you let him read you the Bible's answers to your questions."

"Read from John's Gospel, Selassie; read how Jesus frees from sin," urged Maryam.

"With all my heart," said Selassie, opening his Bible. This is what he read:

> Jesus said, "If you abide in my word, you are truly my disciples, and you will know the truth, and the truth will set you free." They answered him, "We are offspring of Abraham and have never been enslaved to anyone. How is it that you say, 'You will become free'?"
>
> Jesus answered them, "Truly, truly, I say to you, everyone who commits sin is a slave to sin. . . . So if the Son sets you free, you will be free indeed." (John 8:31–36)

"Now read him what the apostle Paul told the Galatians," said Gebre. Selassie turned over a few more pages and read:

> In Christ Jesus you are all sons of God, through faith. . . . And if you are Christ's then you are Abraham's offspring, heirs according to promise. (Galatians 3:26, 29)

"Offspring of Ibrahim!" I exclaimed. "That is what we Arabs are, for we are descendants of Ismail, Ibrahim's son. But we are still slaves of sin, like Jews and Persians and Franks and Indians and Ethiopians and all the other peoples of the world. The Bible is telling me that Jesus frees us from slavery to sin and makes us real sons of Ibrahim. But how does he do that? That is not the work of a prophet, is it?"

"No, Sinbad," replied Selassie, "but Jesus was also a priest. He gave himself as a sacrifice to redeem us from our sins and their guilt. Listen to these words, also from the apostle Paul to the Galatians. And remember, they are really God's word, not Paul's words." Selassie read:

> Christ redeemed us from the curse of the law by becoming a curse for us—for it is written: "Cursed is everyone who is hanged on a tree"—so that in Christ Jesus the blessing of Abraham might come to the Gentiles, so that we might receive the promised Spirit through faith. (Galatians 3:13–14)

"So that is how the Son made Christians free, by redeeming them!" I exclaimed with joy. "Well, I know what redeeming is: it is the purchase of a slave in order to give him his freedom. You did that for me, Gebre. But it only cost you sixty silver sequins. The Bible says that the purchase of a soul cost Jesus his life."

Gebre smiled broadly; then his face became sober. "But do you believe what the Bible says, Sinbad? Do you believe he did it for you? It is by faith in Jesus and his blood that we receive all God offers us."

Gebre went on to tell me how only one who was himself God could pay for sins committed against an infinite God, and only one who was a human being could live a perfect human life and take on himself the penalty of human sin. Jesus was both God and man. "I know that's something hard for Muslims to believe, Sinbad. It's hard for anyone to believe. But God the Father gave proof of it by raising Jesus from the dead. Selassie, read Sinbad Romans 1:3 and 4."

> Concerning his Son, who was descended from David according to the flesh and was declared to be the son of God in power according to the Spirit of holiness by his resurrection from the dead, Jesus Christ our Lord.

Gebre asked again, "Sinbad, do you believe this?"

I remained silent while conflicting thoughts warred in my soul. On the one hand, I knew that what the Bible said was true. But visions of what could happen to me if I allowed myself to embrace it rose up before me and made me hesitate. If I became a Christian, I would have to declare myself openly. But when a Muslim becomes a Christian, he is subject to death. The Caliph might not choose to order my execution, for he had many Christians in his realm whom he tolerated. He might look the other way when he heard I had become a follower of Jesus. But merchants would refuse to do business with me, and friends and family would cut me off and treat me as dead. A few might stand by me, but I could be entirely friendless and alone. Becoming a Christian promised hardship and suffering. On the other hand, I would have new brothers and sisters in the Christian community in Baghdad. Best of all, God promised a crown of life in heaven to those who are faithful. Eternity with God—that settled the matter.

Gebre repeated his question for a third time: "Once more, I ask you, Sinbad, Do you believe this?"

My struggle was over. I would become a Christian. I replied with a calm heart, "Gebre, Maryam, Selassie, even a few weeks ago, I would have told you I didn't believe it. But I've come to see that the Christian faith offers exactly what we poor sinners need, freedom from sin and a place in God's family. As I hear you read the Bible, I find faith in my heart to believe its promises. What must I do to become a Christian and enter into this freedom and into the family of God?"

Tears of joy in his eyes, Selassie answered simply, "If you have the faith, then just ask God to forgive your sins and make you his child because of what Jesus did for you. Go on, bow your head now and ask him to do this, thanking him for what Jesus did for you by living and dying on your behalf."

And that is what I did. We all embraced, laughing and crying at the same time. Then each of my friends prayed in turn for me, asking God to teach me, keep me, increase my faith, and make me a faithful Christian and a blessing to others.

"I know it's getting late," I finally said, "but I have two questions I must ask now. First, where did my faith come from? It can't just be a matter of understanding the Bible, for some *imams* have made a great study of the Bible in order to refute it."

Gebre replied, "God is the author of faith. He uses the Bible to kindle faith. As the Bible itself says, 'faith comes from hearing the message, and the message is heard through the word of Christ.' That's why it was so important to read the Bible to you rather than just tell its teachings in our own words. What's your other question?"

"I must have a Bible of my own to read and study. Where can I get an Arabic Bible?"

"Truly, Sinbad, I don't know," replied Gebre. "I've heard that the Jews have translated some of the Hebrew scriptures into Arabic, but I have never heard of a translation of the New Testament, the part of the Bible that tells us everything we know about Jesus. The New Testament was written in Greek. I don't think it has been turned into Arabic."

"What!" I was astonished. "How do Christians in other lands expect us to learn about Jesus if we don't have a Bible we can read? Don't they care that we perish in our sins?"

"I'm ashamed to say that the Christian world hardly gave the Arabs any thought before Muhammad. They thought of your people as wild desert nomads when they thought of them at all. Later, after the conquests of Islam, Christians under Muslim rule were more concerned with preserving their own skin than loving their new neighbors. They knew that death was the penalty for trying to convert a Muslim to Christ. I blush to admit that many who name the name of Jesus Christ don't have real faith or the heart of love that goes with it."

"Then I must learn Hebrew and Greek and translate the Bible for my people. That is what I will devote my life to when I return to Baghdad. Now that I know the joy and peace of freedom from sin and of being a child of God, I must make the truth of Jesus known to my Arab brothers."

Selassie's face flushed with excitement. "Come with us to Axum, Sinbad! We have scholars there who can teach you to read the Bible in Hebrew and Greek."

I solemnly shook hands with my friends to seal the bargain. Then a new thought occurred to me.

"Selassie, what an ironic thing it is. I'll go with you to Axum, but then I'll probably never see you again. You'll be off looking for your father."

"Why, that's the most wonderful thing of all, Sinbad, apart from you becoming a follower of Christ. I haven't had time to tell you my great news. While staying in the Ethiopian quarter here in Aden, I learned that my father survived the night raid that made me a captive. I sent him word that I was here, and just today, I received a reply. More than a reply—father sent a ship to bring me back to Adulis. We can sail to my homeland together, you and I, with Gebre and Maryam sailing beside us. What a joyful trip that will be!"

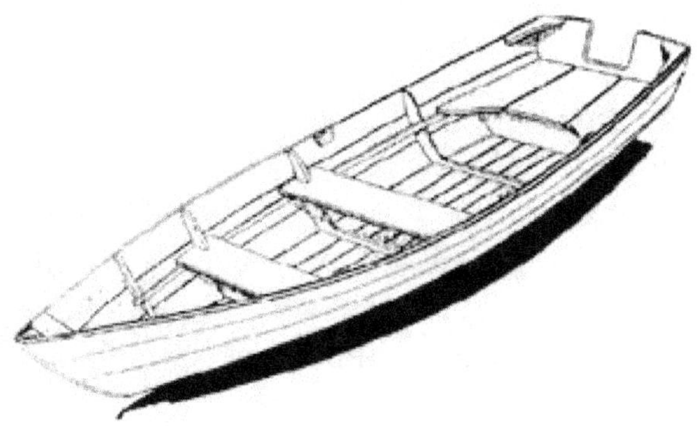

Chapter 26
Old Enemies

We left Aden the next day. The ship that came for Selassie was sleek and fast, too small to sail on the open ocean but well-suited to skirting the shores of the Red Sea. We crossed the Bab al-Mandab to the African side and turned north, keeping the coast in view on the port side. The captain was a tall, thin Ethiopian with a grizzled beard, an experienced sailor who knew both sides of the Red Sea like the back of his hand.

"By my reckoning, we should reach Adulis in a week and a day," the captain said to me. "Selassie's father is so excited, he's probably waiting at the dock already. He's been in the depths of gloom ever since Selassie was carried away. I admit that I'm excited, too—Selassie's my grandnephew, you know. I remember him as a young boy who didn't even come up to my knee; now he's practically as tall as his father." He chattered on until the breeze shifted and he had to go aft to give the helmsman new orders. I remained in the bow, lost in thought.

As the flat, sandy Somali coast slipped by, I meditated on everything that had happened to me since I left Basra. What a change God had worked in my mind and heart!

I thought how time and again Selassie had faced death with a calm I didn't have. He didn't fear the Day of Judgment as I did. That piqued my interest in the Christian faith. Later, Selassie's challenge to the Prophet of the Sun got me thinking about Muhammad in a new way. What had Muhammad done to prove he was a prophet? We Muslims had nothing but Muhammad's word for it that the angel Gabriel spoke to him.

I reflected on our conversation about *qismat*, when I learned that the God of the Bible loved his people before they ever were and would never change his mind about them. The Koran never said that about God. Later, as Selassie spoke with Prince Vishnipim, I first began to doubt that Christians had corrupted the *Injeel*, the gospel of Jesus, as my teachers always claimed. It was then that I first desired to hear about Jesus from the Bible.

Then there was our talk on the way to Allepey, when I first felt a longing to know God as a father and to be his child. Only a day later, in the company of the apes, I learned that we are born sinners.

Maryam, too, helped me on my journey to Christ. It was she who made me understand that we need the righteousness of Christ rather than a righteousness based on our own good works. And Gebre had his part: it was he who first told me that Christ had to die to take away our sins.

God used my own cowardice to convince me completely that I was a sinner. He delivered me from marriage to a pagan; but afterward, I had to admit that I would have gone through with the wedding to save my skin.

And God himself confirmed all the good and wholesome words that Selassie, Maryam, and Gebre spoke to me by rescuing me from so many dangers. Often he saved me in answer to Selassie's prayers.

It wasn't my own wits or good luck that delivered me from death a dozen times over, you can be sure of that! God was patiently working the whole time to prepare me to accept Christ in that little seaside café in Aden.

I must have been musing on these things for an hour when one of Gebre's crew appeared at my side. He had rowed over from Gebre's ship with an invitation for Selassie and me: Would we join them for afternoon tea on his deck?

When we arrived on Gebre's dhow, we found him and Maryam sitting on deck under a canvas awning. He stood to greet us, bidding a deckhand to bring refreshments. Soon we were sitting cross-legged on a fine Persian carpet, drinking tea sweetened with honey from jade-green porcelain cups.

"Gebre, do you have time now to tell me how your ship was delayed in reaching the Red Sea? Selassie and I suffered many mishaps after the giant fish tore us away from you, yet you arrived in Aden after me. Selassie suggests that you had troubles of your own."

"An understatement, Sinbad! Yes, let me tell you everything that befell us. It will give God glory and furnish you some entertainment as well, though I don't mind saying it didn't seem at all entertaining at the time.

"Maryam was so distressed when I told her your ship couldn't possibly find us again! 'Father, what can have happened to them?' she kept asking. 'I'm afraid it's something terrible! Will Selassie ever reach our homeland? Will Sinbad ever see Arabia?'

"'Daughter, how can I know?' I replied. 'We'll have to trust them to God and go on our way.' We knelt in prayer right then and committed you into the Lord's loving, faithful care. And we didn't cease praying daily for you.

"We continued sailing northwest. One morning, as we were plowing through green swells and white foam, a jarring blow struck the keel and knocked our feet out from under us, sending us sprawling on the deck. I thought we'd hit a sunken log, and rushed to the rail to investigate. Looking over the side, I saw the strangest sight I think I've ever seen. The half-submerged remains of a strange craft bobbed up and down beside the dhow. Once it was a large ball made of iron and crystal, but now the iron frame was twisted and bent, and the crystal was shattered. Two men lay unconscious in the wreckage, which was rapidly filling with water.

"'Quickly, Lal, into the water! Rescue those men before they drown,' I yelled to one of my Indian sailors, who was an excellent swimmer.

"Lal jumped into the sea and, with a few powerful strokes, was beside the men. Other sailors cast lines over the side. Lal looped a line under each man's arms. Hand over hand, my brawny crewmen hauled the victims up to the deck.

"We laid them out on this very carpet. The men were unconscious but appeared uninjured. They revived after a few minutes. Maryam gave them strong black tea, and when they had recovered their senses and some strength, we were able to question them. Fortunately, the men knew Arabic, though we could see by their dress they weren't Arabs. What strange clothing!

"One man identified himself as the First Comrade and the other said he was the Second Comrade. That meant nothing to me. They informed us they came from a city undersea. Naturally, I was inclined to doubt their word. But Ganesh, who was on watch when the crash occurred, nodded his head vigorously.

"'They've got to be telling the truth, Captain. I swear by the great god Ganesh, my namesake, there was nothing floating around the ship before we got hit. That outlandish vessel struck us below the waterline, right on the keel. A few seconds later, their craft popped up from the deep.'

"'All right,' I said to the men, 'The evidence supports your claim to come from undersea, remarkable as it is. But why weren't you looking where you were going?'

"To my surprise, the comrades weren't at all ashamed or embarrassed about hitting us. In fact, they angrily accused us of 'running into them,' as they put it. They haughtily demanded my cabin for the rest of the voyage and insisted that we change course for Zanzibar immediately. I shot back that the collision was their fault, that they should be grateful we saved them rather than presuming to order us about, that they would have to sleep on the open deck with the crew, and that I had no intention of going to Zanzibar.

"I was still giving those ingrates a tongue lashing when an Indian sailor named Nil rushed up and breathlessly informed me that the crash had cracked a plank in the hull. We were taking on water. At once, I ordered two of the crew down into the hold to man the bilge pumps. 'And take our two visitors with you,' I added. 'They caused this damage; they can take their turn at the pumps.' The comrades protested violently, but Nil and Lal seized each one by the arm and hustled them away. They were still babbling out orders as they disappeared below deck."

"I know those men, Gebre," I interrupted. "They told you the truth about a city undersea. Selassie and I have been there." Gebre drew in his breath sharply, and Maryam's eyes grew wide as Selassie described the city in the dome and recounted our adventure there.

"The comrades are wicked men," Selassie concluded. "We were able to make the rest of the colony realize that just before we escaped. I guess the comrades escaped too."

"I don't think they escaped," I said. "Didn't you notice how they were black and blue from head to foot? I should think the colonists beat their former leaders within an inch of their lives and then sent them away in exile."

"I couldn't say," replied Gebre. "For the rest of the trip, they wouldn't talk to me or my crew. That didn't bother us. Those proud men spent all their time berating each other. 'This is a fine mess you've gotten us into now, Second Comrade,' the First Comrade would say to his companion. The Second Comrade would retort, 'Oh it's my fault, is it? If you hadn't been so greedy, we'd have gotten away with the jewels.' And so they went on, back and forth, never accepting any blame themselves but putting it on the other. They weren't very good at pumping, either. I imagine they never did a lick of work in their lives. But we did succeed in pumping the hold dry and keeping it that way. We also made a make-shift repair to the damaged planks.

"I altered our course and made for the island of Socotra. The sooner we could repair the hull, the better. Unfortunately, I wasn't familiar with those waters. As we approached Socotra, I found that we were slowing down even though the winds were picking up.

"'Yusuf,' I asked my first mate, 'What's happening? This old tub isn't making even two knots, yet the winds must be at least fourteen knots.'

"'Sir, just look over the side, and you'll see what the problem is.'

"I looked down at the sea and discovered that the dhow was struggling through a thickening bed of yellow seaweed. Even as I stared, our motion through the reedy water ceased. Long ropes of kelp wrapped around the rudder; mats of leafy sargasso pressed in on all sides of the hull. We were stuck.

"I ordered the men over the side to cut a path through the seaweed with their scimitars. 'Make a channel back to where we came from. We'll furl the sails and tow the dhow out of here with our boats.' The crew set to work with vigor. After an hour, they had hacked their way through a hundred yards of matted kelp and were halfway to clear water when we heard a faint cry: 'Help me, please help me!' Someone else was stuck in the weeds!

"All hands looked in the direction of that pitiful voice. There he was, a scant ten yards from us: a single man in a small boat, just as entangled in kelp as we had been.

"'Ahoy there! Can you swim over here?' I called to the man.

"'I can't swim at all,' he replied.

"'We'll throw you a line. Fasten it to your boat, and we'll try to tow you over here.'

"I cast the man a line, and he made it fast to his bow. My crewmen were well-muscled, but even they had to strain and sweat to drag the boat through the reeds. I dropped a ladder to the man, and he climbed up to the deck. When he appeared before me, I received an unpleasant surprise: the man we had saved was Trangaram, the traitorous friend of Prince Vishnipim!

"'You! What are you doing here in the middle of the ocean?'

"Trangaram was as astonished to see me as I was to see him. Was he dismayed to find that the man he had unjustly imprisoned was his rescuer? I suspected so, but whatever his thoughts were, he kept them to himself and addressed me quite respectfully.

"'I thank you profusely for rescuing me, Gebre. I've meditated on my misdeeds much since I was sent away by Prince Vishnipim. I hope you can find it in your heart to forgive me the wrong I did you. I beg you to take me with you wherever you are going.'

"I didn't know whether the man had truly repented or not, but a Christian must forgive his enemies. 'I forgive you freely, Trangaram, as Christ has forgiven me. Of course, you can come with us. But you'll have to do your share of the work like the rest of us.' I extended my hand in friendship.

"Trangaram took my hand and pumped it warmly. 'Gladly, Gebre. Where do I start?'

"I told Yusuf to tell Trangaram his duties and turned back to the task at hand, cutting a channel through the remaining seaweed. The men made good progress, and before evening we were back in open water. As the surface of the ocean rose and fell in gentle swells, we could see the immense mass of seaweed off the port bow, a golden carpet floating on the green, glassy sea. We turned north to give that oceanic swamp a wide berth. We sailed north for a day and a half before we were finally clear of the menacing sargasso; then I ordered the mate to turn west again. I still intended to have the dhow repaired in Socotra.

"Maryam and I normally took our meals apart from the crew. One night after supper, she asked me, 'Father, have you noticed that Trangaram has made friends with the First and Second Comrade? They're always talking together when they're not working. Call it woman's intuition, but I'm sure they can't be up to any good.'

"'No, I hadn't noticed; but that is a matter for concern. If Trangaram really had a change of heart, he would seek better companions. I'll keep an eye on them. You keep an eye on them too.'

"Later that evening, as I was making my rounds of the duty stations, I shared my concerns with Yusuf. He promised to watch them closely.

"That same night, the lights of Socotra came into view. I told the men to strike the sails and let out the anchors. Socotra is surrounded by a coral reef, and I didn't dare try to find the entrance to the harbor in the dark. Just a little to the left or right, and we'd rip a hole in the hull that would send us to the bottom before we knew what happened. We would enter the harbor in the morning.

"I was awakened from a deep sleep by persistent pounding on my cabin door. I opened the door to find Yusuf there. 'Sir, the ship is sinking!' he exclaimed. I pushed past him onto the deck. There was no doubt about it: the ship was riding a good foot lower in the water than when I went to bed.

"I called for a light and plunged into the hold. What a sight met my eyes! Nil and Lal, who had been working the pumps, were trussed up with rope like wild boars captured in the hunt. The water was already up to their chins, but they didn't know it: purple welts on their heads revealed they had been knocked unconscious. Shattered fragments of what had been the bilge pumps floated on the water slowly rising in the hold.

"'Get these men up on deck, quickly!' I shouted to the crewmen who had crowded into the hold with me. When we were all on deck, I mustered the men. Three were missing, and you can guess who: the two comrades and Trangaram. It was all too clear what they had done. As soon as those knaves saw the lights of Socotra, they knocked Nil and Lal over the head, tied them up, destroyed the pumps, and made for shore in one of the boats. I suspected that if we had time to inspect the cargo, we would find that they had taken a bale of silks or spices also. This was to be their revenge: they would reach land, and we would drown. It looked like their dastardly plan would succeed, too, for the dhow was sinking lower, inch by inch, into the dark ocean.

"'If anyone has a good idea how we can stop this tub from going under, now would be a very good time to share it with the rest of us,' I said. 'If not, we'll have to abandon ship. Half of you can take the other boat; the rest will have to float on casks and boxes.'

"'I have an idea, Father,' said Maryam timidly. 'I'm no sailor, but I know how to cook rice. Rice swells up in water. We have a dozen sacks of rice in the galley. Could we fill the cracks in the hull with rice? Maybe it would puff up and stop the water from seeping in.'

"'We'll try it: What do we have to lose? Men, tear your shirts into rags. Roll up rice in the cloths and stuff them into every cleft and crevice that lets water in. When you've done that, form a bucket brigade and try to empty out the hold by hand. We'll know in less than an hour if Maryam's ploy works.'

"I sent four of the men to bring the rice on deck while the other sailors began to rip their garments into strips. Then they all plunged into the hold and went to work, feverishly stuffing rice into every leak.

When they could find no more cracks to plug, they formed a line from the hold up the ladder to the deck and across the deck to the rail. The sailors passed buckets of water from one man to another till the last man dumped his load over the side and sent the empty buckets back to the hold again. For over an hour, my crew bailed for their lives.

"Shortly before dawn, a chorus of cheers from the hold told the rest of us they were making progress. Inch by inch, the water level was going down. 'Stop bailing and rest,' I ordered. 'Let's see if the rice is doing its part.' I went down in the hold and drew a chalk mark at the water line. The men ceased their labors and stood panting while we waited to see if the water would creep up over the line.

"'It's working, men!' I announced after a half hour. 'The leaks are sealed! Finish bailing, then get some rest. We'll enter the lagoon and dock in the city in the morning.'

"While the dog-tired crew shuffled off to their sleeping mats, Maryam and I thanked the Lord for graciously preserving our lives; then we went to bed too.

"I rose at dawn to pray but let the men sleep in till nine o'clock. They had earned their rest. Maryam prepared a big breakfast for everyone, and after the crew ate, they sprang to their duty stations as though nothing had happened the night before—how vigorous are men of the sea!

"The bright morning sun gleamed off the coral reef that surrounded the island entirely except for one dark gap. That would be the passage into the lagoon. We sailed for the gap. I put Nil and Lal in the bow to serve as lookouts and told them to watch for underwater coral. Many a ship has torn its bottom out on a submerged outcropping near a reef.

"'Sir, look to starboard!' Lal shouted as we neared the opening. 'Right on the edge of the reef!' I whistled with astonishment as I saw what Lal had sighted. Our ship's boat, or what was left of it, was impaled on a jagged coral spire standing like a watchtower at the entrance to the harbor. Water sloshed inside the wreckage, and that was all. There was no sign of Trangaram or the comrades. In their hurried flight, they had missed the gap and foundered on the reef.

"'Those wicked men met their *qismat*,' said Yusuf, shaking his head. 'It was their *karma*,' said Nil. 'No,' I replied, 'it wasn't *qismat* or *karma*. God punished them for their wickedness. How glad I am that I didn't raise my hand against them. Christians ought always to leave vengeance to the Lord.'

"Well, Sinbad, there's not much more to tell. The boat wrights in Socotra weren't able to make full repairs to the dhow, but they told me that what we'd done with the rice would serve well until we made Aden. I purchased new bilge pumps, and we proceeded on our way. We reached Aden without further incident. You know the rest of the story."

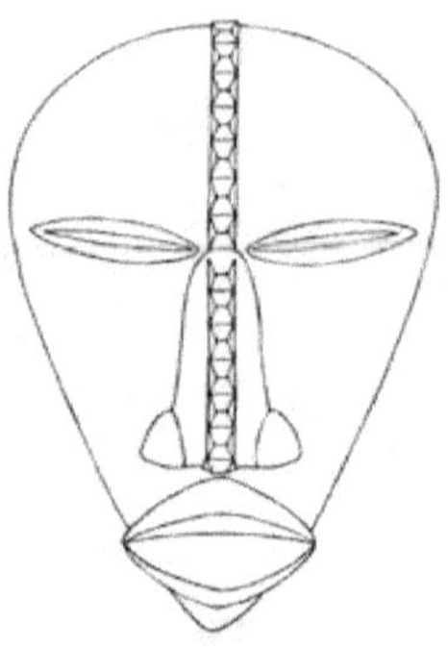

Chapter 27

Unexpected Guests

As a new Christian, I had so much to learn. During the following week, I talked about the things of God with my friends. They taught me how to pray, they read the Bible to me, and they instructed me on how a child of God is to live in this world. I eagerly soaked it all up. For so many years, I had lived in error, in selfishness, in sin. I wanted to make up for lost time by being a light for Christ in Baghdad when I returned.

Sunrise on the eighth day found us in sight of Adulis. "Selassie," I exclaimed, "In just a few hours, you'll be reunited with your loved ones again! What a happy day for you!" My friend was too overwhelmed at the thought of seeing his family to reply, but his broad smile and glistening eyes told me what he felt inside. He had donned the attire of his own country and looked quite striking. I, too, put on my best garments, for I wanted to make a good impression on Selassie's father.

A crowd of ebony-skinned men and women stood on the pier awaiting our arrival. A man in front of the crowd threw Yusuf a line, and he made it fast to a cleat on deck. The man threw a second line, which Yusuf also secured. A third man pushed a ladder against the side of the dhow. Selassie was the first to hurry down the ladder. By the time I set foot on the dock, Selassie had found his family and was bringing them to meet me. A slender man in regal clothing approached and bowed.

Selassie hurried forward to introduce me. "Father, I want you to meet Sinbad, my best friend. He bought me out of slavery and saved me from death at least a dozen times."

We bowed to each other, and Selassie's father addressed me in excellent Arabic. "Welcome to Adulis, Sinbad. My name is Mekonnen. I am the military governor of this province. My boy wrote me a long letter from Aden telling me all about you and your adventures together. I can't begin to repay you for all you've done for my son. I want you to know that I consider you a friend for life. You have but to ask, and I'll do anything in my power."

"Sir," I answered, "Selassie is too kind; but that's his nature. He saved my life on several occasions as well. I've heard a lot about you, too. You can be proud of your son. He proved to be brave, clever, and above all, faithful to the Lord. Selassie has shown himself to be a worthy heir of his noble father."

"Here's my mother, Sinbad, and my brothers and sisters too," interrupted Selassie. We greeted each other warmly. Then Selassie brought Gebre and Maryam forward to meet his family. After the introductions, Mekonnen, Gebre, and Maryam conversed in Geez for a long time. I'd begun to learn Geez, but they spoke so fast that I couldn't make out a word of their conversation.

When everyone had been introduced to everyone else, Mekonnen gave orders that the weary travelers should be conducted to his residence in an old fort overlooking the harbor. "Your rooms are already prepared. Refresh yourselves. After you've lunched, bathed, and napped, my orderlies will show you around the town. Tonight we'll feast in celebration of my son's return."

I needed the rest. I hadn't realized how tired my body was till I lay down on those silken sheets for just a catnap. I fell asleep at once and slept all afternoon. An orderly had to knock loudly on my door to rouse me. I opened my eyes to see that the sun had nearly set.

"Beg your pardon, sir, but the banquet begins in a half hour. Selassie thought you would want to be awakened." I rose quickly and dressed for dinner. My friends were waiting outside my door when I stepped into the hall. Selassie had grown up in the fort and knew every twisting and turning of its corridors. He led us straight to the regimental mess hall, which had been decorated specially for the banquet.

"Father says some other travelers will also dine with us," Selassie said as he opened the door to the mess hall. "Apparently, they're a trade delegation from a far country. I'm curious to meet them." When we entered the mess hall, the stewards showed us to our places at the head table. Selassie's family was already seated. Bowing low, Gebre, Maryam, and I sat where Mekonnen indicated. There were still a dozen empty seats at the table for the other diners.

We barely had time to exchange pleasantries when the doors opened again and the honored travelers entered the room. Imagine my astonishment when I saw who they were: the Axumite chief and his officers, the very men who had intended to sell us into slavery! They were as surprised to see me as I was to see them. We eyed each other warily as they sat down across the table from us.

"Sinbad, Gebre, Maryam: I want you to meet some special travelers," Mekonnen said. "These men are long-lost countrymen of mine. For three hundred years, they've lived in an Ethiopian colony on an island in the middle of the Indian Ocean. Their ancestors were blown off course in a great storm. You may know that we Ethiopians aren't great sailors, and how they came to be at sea in the first place is a long story I won't bother you with now. Until recently, they didn't know how to build ships or sail. Happily, earlier this year, a shipwrecked mariner helped them build a fleet and taught them to sail. So now, at last, they have been able to find their way home."

"Really!" I exclaimed with a grin. "Where is this mariner? He must be the most esteemed guest of all. Tell me, travelers, where is your benefactor? Did he sail with you? Is he present at table tonight?"

The Axumite chief looked at me with dread in his eyes. Was I about to reveal his ungrateful treachery to Governor Mekonnen? After a minute of dead silence, he replied in an unsteady voice: "Sir, I'm sorry to say that his ship became separated from ours a few hundred miles from Aden."

"I hope he wasn't lost at sea," I replied. "That would be a sad ending for a man you surely wanted to honor with gifts and praise for his goodness to you. Tell me, Captain, how did you plan to reward this man?"

Again the Axumite leader hesitated, then replied: "We discovered only today that he wasn't lost at sea but arrived safely at his destination."

I pressed on with my questioning: "And his reward? Do you plan to do something grand for him? I'm sure Governor Mekonnen would like to honor him too. And if you don't have the means to fulfill your good intentions, just say the word. The governor told me he'd do anything I asked if it was in his power. He'll do good to those who've done good to me and punish those who've done me wrong. I'm sure he'll do the same to you." As I said these words, I stared straight at the captain. He looked away.

I was thinking of how best to expose the evil of the men who had schemed to sell me into slavery, how best to get my revenge, when I glanced at Selassie. Never had he looked so sad. I looked over at Gebre and Maryam. Gebre's eyes were downcast; Maryam was softly weeping. Why? Weren't they happy that these wicked men were about to be revealed for what they were and to be severely punished by Mekonnen?

Then I remembered. Christians don't seek revenge; Christians show mercy. They forgive as Christ forgave them. Gebre had shown mercy to Trangaram, who had held him unjustly in prison for three long years. More to the point, Christ had shown mercy to me. I remembered the Lord's Prayer, which Gebre taught me and which we said every night together before bed: *forgive us our debts, as we forgive our debtors*. The Lord had added the warning that if we don't forgive those who sin against us, he will not forgive our sins. I knew what I had to do.

"Well, enough of this talk," I said with a wave of my hand. "I rejoice with you that you've returned to the land of your fathers, and I hope you can come and go often. As a matter of fact, I know the man who helped you. He wasn't a follower of Jesus when you knew him, but he became one in Aden. God forgave him, and he learned to forgive his enemies. If he hadn't sailed with you, he wouldn't have come to Aden; maybe then he wouldn't have become a Christian. I know he's grateful he sailed with you even though our ships got separated on the way. I can assure you that he's very happy for you, too, and wishes you many blessings in Christ. So then, tell me all about your island home."

The chief's strained face relaxed, and he smiled faintly. "I'm relieved to hear that the man who helped us so much reached port. I'm even happier he became a Christian. I have to admit I haven't been a very faithful Christian myself, but your words make me want to renew my allegiance to Jesus. Thank you for that, Sinbad, thank you." I reached across the table and shook the man's hand. We were reconciled.

The other Axumites were deeply moved by my forgiveness (so small compared with what God forgave me!) and their chief's repentance. As we celebrated Selassie's homecoming around the banquet table, we warmed up to each other. In fact, to my surprise, we found ourselves becoming friends. I was beginning to know first-hand the truth that Christ reconciles us to each other when he reconciles us to God.

I don't know if Selassie ever told his father the story of the Axumites' treachery; I doubt it. God forgets our sins and remembers them no more, and we should do the same with the sins our enemies commit against us. And if we forget them, we shouldn't talk about them.

I had overcome one temptation, the first of many in my new Christian life. I wouldn't always resist temptation successfully, but I came to learn that if I was watchful in prayer, temptation couldn't sneak up on me unawares and unprepared. And I learned that I could overcome temptation in the strength God supplies.

*****

There's no more to tell about my eighth voyage, for I never set foot on a deck again. I made my way back to Baghdad on dry land. I said my farewells to Gebre and Maryam in Adulis and traveled with Mekonnen and Selassie up to the highlands of Ethiopia. They left me in the city of Axum after solemnly promising to visit me in Baghdad in two years' time. It was hard saying goodbye to Selassie, but I knew for sure that the Lord would keep watch over both of us till we met again in my home.

In Axum, I spent a year studying Hebrew and Greek, the original languages of the Bible. There I was able to purchase copies of the Hebrew and Greek Scriptures, as well as a Geez Bible—I had become quite fluent in Geez by then, for it is distantly related to Arabic. From Axum, I traveled down the Blue Nile to Khartoum, then down the Nile all the way to Alexandria. In Alexandria, I joined a caravan that took me to Jerusalem, Damascus, and Edessa before reaching Mosul, in northern Mesopotamia. From Mosul, I could have taken a boat down the Tigris River to Baghdad, but I'd had enough of sailing to last a lifetime. The ship of the desert was the only ship I wanted to ride. I bought a camel and plodded south over the fertile, well-watered Mesopotamian plain until I came at last to Baghdad. I was home.

I arrived home with a priceless treasure. No, not gold or pearls. Seven times I returned from over the ocean with such baubles. But I always went to sea again, for I always wanted more. This time I came back satisfied with my treasure. I would sail the seven seas no more, for the wide world offered nothing to compare with what I had obtained on my eighth voyage. I now had the treasure of peace with God, the righteousness of Christ, a heavenly Father, and eternal life!

www.ingramcontent.com/pod-product-compliance
Lightning Source LLC
Chambersburg PA
CBHW070352200726
48294CB00003B/871
9781960297006